## Maurice Procter and The Murder Room

**⟩⟩⟩** This title is part of The Murder Room, our series dedicated to making available out-of-print or hard-to-find titles by classic crime writers.

Crime fiction has always held up a mirror to society. The Victorians were fascinated by sensational murder and the emerging science of detection; now we are obsessed with the forensic detail of violent death. And no other genre has so captivated and enthralled readers.

Vast troves of classic crime writing have for a long time been unavailable to all but the most dedicated frequenters of second-hand bookshops. The advent of digital publishing means that we are now able to bring you the backlists of a huge range of titles by classic and contemporary crime writers, some of which have been out of print for decades.

From the genteel amateur private eyes of the Golden Age and the femmes fatales of pulp fiction, to the morally ambiguous hard-boiled detectives of mid twentieth-century America and their descendants who walk our twenty-first century streets, The Murder Room has it all. **⟩⟩⟩**

## The Murder Room
### Where Criminal Minds Meet

**themurderroom.com**

T0352377

**Maurice Procter 1906–1973**

Born in Nelson, Lancashire, Maurice Procter attended the local grammar school and ran away to join the army at the age of fifteen. In 1927 he joined the police in Yorkshire and served in the force for nineteen years before his writing was published and he was able to write full-time. He was credited with an ability to write exciting stories while using his experience to create authentic detail. His procedural novels are set in Granchester, a fictional 1950s Manchester, and he is best known for his series characters, Detective Superintendent Philip Hunter and DCI Harry Martineau. Throughout his career, Procter's novels increased in popularity in both the UK and the US, and in 1960 *Hell is a City* was made into a film starring Stanley Baker and Billie Whitelaw. Procter was married to Winifred, and they had one child, Noel.

**Philip Hunter**

The Chief Inspector's Statement (1951)
  aka *The Pennycross Murders*
I Will Speak Daggers (1956)
  aka *The Ripper*

**Chief Inspector Martineau**

Hell is a City (1954)
  aka *Somewhere in This City*
The Midnight Plumber (1957)
Man in Ambush (1958)
Killer at Large (1959)

Devil's Due (1960)
The Devil Was Handsome (1961)
A Body to Spare (1962)
Moonlight Flitting (1963)
   aka *The Graveyard Rolls*
Two Men in Twenty (1964)
Homicide Blonde (1965)
   aka *Death has a Shadow*
His Weight in Gold (1966)
Rogue Running (1966)
Exercise Hoodwink (1967)
Hideaway (1968)

**Standalone Novels**
Each Man's Destiny (1947)
No Proud Chivalry (1947)
The End of the Street (1949)
Hurry the Darkness (1952)
Rich is the Treasure (1952)
   aka *Diamond Wizard*
The Pub Crawler (1956)
Three at the Angel (1958)
The Spearhead Death (1960)
Devil in Moonlight (1962)
The Dog Man (1969)

# The Devil Was Handsome

Maurice Procter

An Orion book

Copyright © Maurice Procter 1960

The right of Maurice Procter to be identified as the author of this work
has been asserted in accordance with the Copyright, Designs and Patents
Act 1988.

This edition published by
The Orion Publishing Group Ltd
Orion House
5 Upper St Martin's Lane
London WC2H 9EA

An Hachette UK company
A CIP catalogue record for this book is available from the British Library

ISBN 978 1 4719 0273 4

www.orionbooks.co.uk

# ONE

'WHAT's this?' demanded Detective Sergeant Devery.

'It's what they call a minute,' the C.I.D. clerk explained kindly. 'Addressed to you.'

'I can see that. I wonder whose tomfool idea this is?'

The clerk looked round in simulated terror. 'Shush,' he said. 'Some very senior officer, I don't doubt.'

'And what does he think he's going to gain by it?'

'Some of our most conservative seniors have not yet admitted that policewomen are on the strength. He thinks he's saving the services of one detective officer.'

'And crippling me by giving me a woman to carry around,' growled Devery. 'What a profession!'

He looked up, and saw the grinning faces of detectives Cook, Cassidy and Ducklin. He ignored them while he perused the minute again. It was from Chief Superintendent Clay, the boss of the C.I.D., but he knew that he would have to look higher than that to find the real author. He suspected the First A.C.C. The prowl cars had been his idea originally. It would be like him to suggest to the Chief that a car with a man and a woman in it would never be spotted as a police vehicle. To assist a detective sergeant a trained woman would be just as good as a man, he would say. And by employing a policewoman for this work, one man would be saved for general C.I.D. duties. As an experiment, of course, sir. A temporary measure, if you like.

Devery knew all about the A.C.C.'s temporary measures. They went on and on, through the summer and the winter too. Which meant that this curse would descend upon Devery for one fortnight every six months. Today was the

Friday of his first week on the prowl. With Sunday off, he had to spend the next eight working days in the company of a woman whom he had not yet seen. Eight hours a day for eight days with a serious-minded policewoman! He scowled at the thought.

The others saw the scowl. Cook opened the bowling. 'I must say they picked the best-looking lad in the division for the job,' he said solemnly.

'And him a bachelor,' Cassidy remarked in his best brogue. 'I'm hoping he don't get the ginger-haired one wid a face like the map of Belfast.'

'He'll be running out of petrol in a dark lane,' sniggered Ducklin.

'That's enough from you lot,' said Devery, not angry with the men. They were behaving as he had expected. He would have to put up with that sort of thing until the novelty wore off.

He told Ducklin, who had been his working companion until today, to go and get his car and bring it round to the front of the building. He stayed for a few minutes looking at the occurrence book, then he went out to the car. Ducklin handed it into his charge with unusual formality, his face wooden. That was because of the girl who stood there. Devery understood him perfectly, being able to imagine how he would soon be bursting into the C.I.D. with his news.

Whether or not the best-looking man in the division had been chosen for this first mixed patrol, the inspector in charge of policewomen must surely have chosen her best-looking girl. Devery did not realize that this choice was not accidental. The lady inspector liked to declare that she trusted all her girls within reasonable limits, but she had also been heard to say that in the matter of *amour* she would not trust a C.I.D. man as far as she could throw a Diesel locomotive. Furthermore, in this instance the inspector had a lively awareness of the dangers of pro-pinquity. If the experiment was to be continued, the smartest and loveliest girl in the force would have to take her turn on the prowl sometime. That being so, it was safer to give her her turn when she would be teamed with one of the few unmarried men in the Criminal Investigation Department. Then if human nature did assert itself, if the worst came to the worst, and so forth, at least there would not be an angry or heartbroken wife to complicate matters. The lady inspector was a very wise lady.

The chosen girl was of medium height, that is to say rather small for a policewoman. She had a good figure, a pretty face, a healthy pallor, brown eyes and brown hair. So why had Ducklin been behaving like an idiot? Devery asked himself the question and perceived the answer while he was looking at the girl. The more you looked the more you saw. The medium-sized figure promised an incomparable vitality and grace; the face was perfectly moulded; the eyes were unusually large, limpid and appealing; the the skin was flawless, of a translucence which revealed an inner glow; the hair was really brown, a warm nut-brown. The girl's neat suit did not disguise her perfection, and the flat-heeled shoes could not mar the shapeliness of her legs.

She stood, a little uncertain about this new experience; slightly nervous perhaps, and slightly embarrassed. Her big eyes were fixed on the man who was to be her partner. A little late, he realized that she was no more pleased with the partnership than he was. She was not the sort to build it up into a romance before it started. Probably she already had a young man. Well, that was all right. He already had a girl.

'I'm Sergeant Devery,' he said.

'Yes, I know,' she replied. 'My name is Valentine.'

'What other name have you?'

The clear skin showed a touch of colour. 'Rosamund.'

He started a grin and changed it into a smile. 'Two nice names,' he said. 'Do I call you Rosamund or Valentine?'

Her glance was level. The big eyes were not at all appealing. 'You call me Valentine, Sergeant.'

'So it's going to be that way, eh? Man to man.'

3

'You do your job, and I'll do mine.'

'Fair enough. Have you passed the Advanced Driving Course, Valentine?'

'No, Sergeant. Just the ordinary police course.'

Devery waved towards the car. 'A bit more practice won't do you any harm,' he said. 'You be the wheelman.'

.　　　.　　　.　　　.　　　.

That meeting occurred at two o'clock on Friday afternoon, the beginning of a two-to-ten tour of duty. But, though it was a form of patrol duty, it was still C.I.D. work, and Devery and the girl understood that they would be lucky if they were able to sign off at ten o'clock and go home.

The prowl cars were new ones, battleship-grey Jaguars. There were two, set aside for their specific purpose. They were 'floaters', augmenting the Area Patrol cars and the men on the beats, the difference being that they did not look like police vehicles. It was hoped, too, that their occupants would not look like police personnel. Each car had half the city for its territory; half the business and shopping districts, half the warehouses and factories, half the docks, half the inner suburbs of soot-blackened brick rows of workers' houses, half the clean outer suburbs and half the residential districts within the city boundary. So far, Devery's car was the only one which carried a woman.

Devery and the fair Rosamund prowled conscientiously throughout the afternoon and early evening, and by eight o'clock they knew all about each other's birthplace and schooldays.

At nine o'clock Devery remarked cautiously: 'It looks as if we're going to get away with it.'

At twenty-five minutes past nine the car's duplex radio gave tongue: 'British Medicaments Ltd.,' it rasped. 'The watchman says he's got thieves in. Any cars near there?'

Devery was driving the Jaguar. 'Tell him it's ours,' he said, putting on speed. 'We'll be there in three minutes.'

'Attention by P.C.P. One, Sergeant Devery and P.W.

Valentine,' the girl crisply told Headquarters. 'Give us three minutes.'

At that time, an hour before the theatres, cinemas and public houses closed for the day, the city streets were comparatively clear of traffic. Making the most of the car's notable acceleration and braking power, Devery required less time than the three minutes Rosamund had asked for. Even so, as he listened to the voice of Headquarters issuing instructions to other cars, he doubted if he would be first on the scene of the crime.

The Granchester warehouse of British Medicaments stood among other warehouses in a business district close to two main railway stations. The high rectangular buildings were set in streets which were all straight lines, with corners which were all right angles. The buildings had no yards. Doors opened straight on to the street, and each warehouse had loading bays which ran deep into the building. At night, with all doors locked and the big roller doors of the loading bays made secure, there was not much cover for a loiterer. To the uniformed men who policed the area on foot, that beat was considered to be 'a doddle'.

Devery's headlights swept the short, straight streets, and his tyres screamed as he took the ninety-degree corners. His destination, Arundel Street, was deserted. Except for a small light in the general office, the B.M. factory was dark and quiet. As Devery stopped the Jaguar, an Area Patrol car pulled up behind it.

He was greatly relieved to see the two men from the A.P. car. Now at least he could keep all exits from the building under surveillance. He turned to the men and pointed. 'You there, and you there,' he said tersely. 'Watch two sides each. I'll try and find how they got in.'

The men knew what to do. They went off, each to a corner of the building. Devery, with Rosamund beside him, went straight to the main office door. It was locked, and the light of his torch revealed that it was unmarked. Though he had the place 'surrounded', he was afraid that he might still have a problem when he discovered the point of entry. Assuming that the watchman's message was not a false alarm due to a mistaken interpretation of a noise, thieves were *inside* the building. What were they seeking? Money from the office, or stock from the warehouse itself? That all depended on whether they were wide boys or mugs. If the thieves were in the stock-rooms, they probably would be wide boys who knew exactly what they wanted. They would not be seeking money in the premises of a firm which dealt mainly with manufacturers and wholesalers. But a backward boy, a mug, would assume that a big concern must have a lot of cash on the premises. Mugs had television ideas about crime. They had notions about the toughness they ought to display in emergencies, and they were inclined to act without regard for consequences. Devery did not greatly fancy leading a woman to an encounter with such men. Something would have to be done to keep her out of harm's way. This was a situation which the A.C.C. had not visualized.

As he moved along the front of the building, examining doors and windows, Devery pondered briefly about thieves and British Medicaments. In a factory full of medicines and the raw materials of medicines, what was there to attract thieves? Undoubtedly this was one of those jobs where the plunder was sold before it was stolen. But what? How much did the thieves intend to take away? What weight of material?

The last question made the sergeant pause at the great steel door of a loading bay. It was secured on the inside, he discovered. Getting down on hands and knees, he laid his cheek on cool, gritty concrete and tried to look under the door. He could not see much. There was a light, but it was faint and distant. Probably it was a small bulb left burning all night to illuminate the loading platform. He sniffed, and detected the garage smell. There was a van, or a number of vans, parked in the bay beside the platform. The thieves might be able to roll up the door and drive a van out of there, loaded with stolen goods.

6

He got to his feet and looked around. Another A.P. car was arriving.

'Valentine,' he said. 'See that car? Tell the crew I want it parked right here across this doorway, as close to the building as they can get. I want to block it, see? Then I want the men to go to the two uncovered corners of the building. Then I want you to get the Jag and block that other loading door. Got it?'

'Yes, Sergeant,' said Rosamund, and she sped away.

Devery resumed his inspection of the building, paying particular attention to basement gratings. When the girl rejoined him he had worked his way round to the rear, and he was stooping over the circular metal cover of a fuel chute. The cover was let into the pavement beside the building. He raised it, and replaced it. He was pleased. Here was a duty for P.W. Valentine. It would keep her occupied, and keep her safe.

'It looks like a mugs' job,' he said. 'They found they could raise this lid, and they went in to see what they could find. They might try to come out this way. I want you to stand on the lid, and if you feel anybody trying to lift it, blow your whistle.'

He went on his way and completed his circuit, and then he waited at the front door for the keys to arrive. Everything was under control. The thieves could not get out of the building without being seen, and minute by minute more police officers were arriving to make the trap more secure. Headquarters would have looked up the address for keys, and some under-manager would be arriving to unlock a door and let the police into the premises without a lot of noise.

Left standing on the iron cover, Rosamund could be clearly seen in the light of street lamps by the two policemen who were stationed at the rear corners of the building. She suspected that she had been put there to be kept out of mischief, but she was determined to do as she had been told, and not disgrace the women police. She was rather more excited than Devery because she also suspected that this was not an ordinary crime. Mugs' job, indeed! What would a thief want from British Medicaments Ltd.? Drugs, of course. The East had its opium and the West its heroin, but in England there was not enough use of the narcotic under either name for it to be a social menace. And information concerning traffic in drugs derived from the poppy seldom came to the ears of the rank and file of the British police. Consequently the ordinary officer was inclined to assume that such traffic was virtually non-existence in his district. To a practical thief-taker like Devery the thought of opium had not occurred. 'He's too much down-to-earth,' mused Rosamund, who already had some respect for the sergeant's acumen. 'Well, he'll know soon enough what this is.'

While she stood meditating at her post, she heard the unmistakable metallic rumble of a big roller door. There was a shout, and then a crash which made her shudder. 'There goes our lovely Jaguar,' she thought. 'We'll be prowling on foot next week.' She noticed that the policemen on the corners did not move from their positions.

Two or three minutes passed, and then some strong person began to press upward on Rosamund's cover. The thieves, baulked in their attempt to escape in a B.M. van, had rushed through the building to try and get out at the point of entry. The cover moved slightly, and the girl began to fear that someone below was strong enough to lift both herself and the lid. She remembered her instructions, and blew her whistle.

The two policemen at the corners, who were probably wondering what she was doing there anyway, could only see a woman who appeared to be blowing a police whistle for no reason at all. Nevertheless, their training demanded that at least one of them must answer the call. One of them did, at a rather bored jog-trot. He assumed quite logically that Rosemary had given way to unreasoning panic. 'Steady, steady,' he said when he arrived. 'Don't get 'ysterical.'

Rosamund pointed down at her feet. 'Somebody just

tried to raise this lid,' she said. 'This is the way they went in.'

'Stand aside,' the constable said. 'Let's have a look.'

Rosamund moved. The P.C. lifted the cover and directed the beam of his flashlight into the chute. 'Nobody there now,' he said gruffly. 'I wonder if I ought to go in.'

'I wouldn't,' Rosamund advised. 'I'd wait for instructions.'

'Happen you're right,' the man said, after some thought. 'I'll put this lid back and get back to me corner.'

He replaced the cover. 'Happen we'd a-caught 'em climbing out if you hadn't been stood on the lid,' he said.

'Sorry,' the girl said without contrition. 'Orders.'

'Ah,' the man began, but the rest of his remark was lost. A great crash of glass was followed by a tinkling shower of falling fragments. The broken window was about thirty yards away, near the corner which the P.C. had just vacated. The window-sill was some six feet from the ground, and poised on the sill was a darkly clad figure with a face which appeared to be white and featureless. The man jumped to the ground and ran.

'Godammit,' said the P.C., and he pounded in pursuit, followed at a distance of fifty yards by the policeman from the other corner.

Other policemen would soon be arriving at the scene of the break-out, Rosamund knew. She walked to the window, and stared curiously at the damage. A masked man appeared in the window, and a cardboard carton landed at her feet. The man stood on the window-sill and jumped, and Rosamund moved to get between him and the carton. He came to brush her aside, a big, strong, active man who thought nothing of a girl's opposition. She got the correct hold of lapel and sleeve and should have thrown him, but it is one thing for a girl to throw a smiling instructor on a wrestling-mat, and quite another thing to throw an unchivalrous heavyweight in a hurry. Moreover, the man was a wrestler. Rosamund never knew exactly what happened, but she flew through the air and landed with no breath in her body. The man picked up the carton and ran away.

As she struggled to raise herself, Rosamund watched the man's departure. Someone passed her at speed, following the man and gaining a little. It was Devery. He had a nice action. 'He'll get a shock when he catches him,' the girl decided. She was not too pleased with the sergeant. A girl typical of her class and generation, she was inclined to measure a man by the yardstick of success. Devery's arrangements had not been wholly effective.

An Area Patrol car turned the corner and stopped beside her. She got to her feet, and looked at the two grinning faces in the car. 'Just having a rest?' one of them asked.

'Get on!' she snapped. 'There are two big men. Running. That way. Get busy with your radio.'

The car went away, with the driver's mate already speaking to Headquarters. A cordon would be formed around the neighbourhood. A little late, Rosamund thought.

She went to the nearest street light and raised her skirt to look at her legs. Her sheer stockings were ruined, but the skin of her knees was not seriously abraded. Her suit was not torn, but it was scuffed and dirty. She felt as if she had bruises all over her body.

'Well, if that's what they call police work,' she said aloud, 'give me a job chasing naughty girls, any time.'

# TWO

ROSAMUND went round to the front of the building. Several uniformed bobbies had arrived. They did not know what was happening, and there was nobody to tell them what to do. They stood in a group near a loading bay, where an A.P. car had been damaged when the thieves had tried to push it out of the way with a three-ton van.

The policewoman was concerned about her appearance; perhaps unnecessarily concerned, since it was dark. 'They'll be able to see that I've been knocked about a bit,' she thought ruefully. 'I look like one of the original ruins. I met Cromwell in person.'

It was a legitimate occupation risk, she presumed. Opposed by this masked character, she had tried to give him the works according to the book, but he had thrown her half the length of the street. Well, it wasn't her fault that he had turned out to be a Black Belt and three Dans.

She went to look at the damaged car, and was thankful that it was not the Jaguar which had suffered. None of the policemen knew her. They eyed her without curiosity, assuming that she was passing by. Presently, no doubt, one of them would have spoken to her.

Any such intention was baulked by the arrival of another police vehicle. It was a C.I.D. car without a 'Police' sign, and out of it stepped three men in plain clothes. One of them was Chief Inspector Martineau, head of the divisional C.I.D.

Martineau was a very big man in a good grey suit and a grey hat carelessly worn. His face was rock hard, but handsome in its way. Within the force he was liked, admired and feared, because he was a likeable man with an admirable and fearsome reputation. It was a reputation well earned, and he was still quite capable of living up to it.

When he approached the group of constables they stiffened to attention. He saw Rosamund and did not know her, but he automatically raised his hat. His blond hair, shot with grey, looked silvery under the street lights.

'Is something happening here, or nothing?' he asked mildly.

'It seems to have happened, sir,' a P.C. replied.

'Ah. The thieves have been arrested?'

'No, sir. They seem to have got away.'

'And you're standing here waiting for them to come back?'

'*I've* only just got here, sir,' the man replied hastily.

'Have we any descriptions?'

Rosamund spoke up, and all the men turned to look at her in astonished silence. 'Two men,' she said. 'Both big and burly, with dark suits, grey cloth caps and their faces covered with white handkerchiefs. One of them will be carrying a cardboard carton.'

'Thank you, young lady,' Martineau said. 'Stay behind for a moment, will you, please? Go back to your beats, men, and see if you can turn up any likely clients.'

The men dispersed. Martineau said to Rosamund: 'Did you witness this affair?'

'I witnessed some of it, sir. I'm a policewoman.'

'Oh, you are?' Martineau was surprised. He refrained from saying something complimentary, and asked: 'Did you happen to be passing when it happened?'

'No, sir. I'm on plain-clothes duty.' Rosamund told him what she knew about the break-in. He and his two men listened in silence until the end.

Then Martineau said: 'Ducklin, perhaps you had better go round to the back and watch the broken window and the manhole cover until we get everything boarded up and secured.'

Ducklin went away. Martineau had been studying the policewoman while she talked, and now he said: 'You had a shaking. Are you all right? Cassidy here can take you to hospital to make sure.'

'No, sir, please. You wouldn't send a man to hospital because he'd been in a bit of a fight. I'd like to stay on duty and sign off with my partner.'

The chief inspector showed neither approval nor disapproval.

'Very well, if you're sure you're all right,' he said. 'It wasn't your fault a big fellow like that was too much for you. Did you say Devery was gaining on him?'

'Oh, he was. Definitely.'

'He's here now,' said Cassidy.

They turned to look. Devery was approaching, carrying a carton. He was limping, and flesh was visible where one leg of his trousers was torn at the knee.

'How far did he throw *you?*' Martineau asked.

'I didn't get to grips,' the sergeant answered ruefully. 'I caught up with him all right. I was just getting ready for the tackle when he dropped this box at my feet. I fell over it. Took a real tumble. He gained enough ground to escape into Bishopsgate and lose himself in the crowd.'

'Too bad. Is that the stolen property?'

'I suppose so. I haven't examined it yet.'

'We'll look at it when we've located the watchman,' said Martineau, turning to peer into the dimness of the loading bay. 'It looks as if it might be narcotics.'

So, Rosamund thought, the possibility of drugs hadn't escaped Martineau, not for a moment. She looked at Devery. That young man was concealing his surprise very well. 'Yes, sir, that's what I thought,' he said.

Two A.P. men arrived, and made sad noises as they looked at their car. 'Never mind,' said Cassidy kindly, 'I'll buy you another one.'

Like Devery, the two men had lost their quarry in Bishopsgate. Martineau heard their story, then left them standing by their car while he led the way into the building. There were three B.M. vans in the bay, and just enough room for a man to walk beside them to reach the steps to the loading platform. The dim light was burning beside an open door which led to an interior corridor. This also was dimly lighted. On each side of it were the doors of stockrooms. Martineau turned in the direction of the general office.

The door to the big room was standing wide open. The policemen stood in the doorway and looked around. The place was quiet, and there was nobody about. Everything appeared to be in order, the long desks shining under a central light.

'Hello!' Martineau called.

Almost at once somebody started banging on a door. 'I'm here! Let me out!' a cracked voice shouted.

They located the voice, and found the watchman by unlocking the door of a windowless storeroom. A little old goblin of a man emerged grinning. 'Police?' he asked.

'Yes,' Martineau replied.

'Ar. I dropped off to sleep after they locked me in there. I can't keep awake in pitch dark, never could. The light switch is outside the door here, see? Did you collar 'em?'

'Not yet, unfortunately.'

'Ar well, I dialled nine-nine-nine, right enough. I thought you'd get 'em.'

'What happened exactly?'

The old eyes twinkled. The watchman looked at Rosamund and winked mischievously. He chose to address his story to her. 'You don't catch a weasel asleep, love,' he said. 'See that open fanlight over the door, an' the light at back of it?'

Smiling, Rosamund admitted that she could see the fanlight.

'Ar, well, I'm sittin' in me corner over there an' I see that light start swingin' just a bit, an' I know somebody has opened a door somewhere. Draughty buildin', this is. Well, I gets up an' has a peep. I saw a big chap along the passage, nosin' into one of the rooms. He didn't see me, so I gets on the phone, nine-nine-nine. I'd just got me message through when two of 'em comes in here. They didn't know

14

I'd phoned, because I'm reckonin' to sit in me corner as if I knew nothin'. One of 'em sees me an' comes over to me. "'Evenin', Grandad," he ses. "Keep quiet an' do as you're told, an' you'll be all right." '

'What was the other man doing?' Martineau asked.

'He was lookin' round. He found the storeroom, an' he called out: "This'll do." So this other chap just gets me by the arm an' walks me to the storeroom, an' they locked me in. I never said a word to 'em. Not one word.'

'You did well to get your message through. Can you describe these men?'

'They were just two big men with white hankies tied across their faces.'

'How big?'

'They were both about the same size. As big as you, they were.'

'How were they dressed?'

'Decent dark suits, not ragged or dirty at all. Cloth caps darkish grey. I think their shoes were black.'

'Gloves?'

'Eeh, I never noticed.'

'Did you get any impression of a definite age?'

'No, I can't say as I did. They were both full-grown, an' young enough to be spry.'

'You heard them speak. Did they sound like local men?'

The watchman thought about that. His lips moved as he sought to recall the shape of certain words. 'I couldn't tell you if they was local,' he said at last. 'The one who spoke to me, he spoke middlin' good, but he weren't a toff. No Eton an' Oxford about him. But where he did come from, I couldn't tell you. He could even a-been American. Now I come to think on it, he did sound a bit like a 'Merican. Or happen he was just tryin' to crack on he was American.'

Martineau nodded. 'He wouldn't be the first to do that. They all think they can talk like Yanks these days.' He put his hand on the carton, which Devery had placed on a desk. 'This is what they were trying to get away with. I don't think there was anything else. Open it, Devery, and let's see what they were after.'

The double lid of the carton was held by a thick rubber band. 'Inner tube,' said Devery, as he pulled it away. 'I wonder if they brought it with them.'

He opened the carton and pulled out a great handful of paper packing. Then he looked inside, and said: 'A lot of little white packets.' He reached into the carton and brought out a neatly labelled package. He read the label. 'Diamorphine. What's that?'

'It's another name for heroin,' said Martineau crisply. 'Is it *all* diamorphine?'

Devery began to lift out the packages and lay them in orderly rows, label upwards, on the desk. There were forty-seven packages, with identical labels.

'About an ounce apiece,' said Martineau. 'That's an awful lot of heroin.'

'It looks as if they were goin' to clean us out of that stuff,' the watchman commented.

Somewhere a door banged. Confident footsteps could be heard. An alert-looking man of middle age appeared in the doorway. He looked at the policemen and at Rosamund, and then he spoke to the watchman. 'Now then, Bernard, what you been doing?' he demanded cheerfully.

'This is Mr. Stenson, our warehouse manager,' said the watchman. 'Mr. Stenson, this is the police.'

Stenson came forward, his glance on the rows of white packages. 'Yes, they told me we'd had burglars,' he said. He looked at Martineau. 'Did they get away with much?'

The chief inspector was rueful. 'As far as we know, they got away with nothing. But they got away.'

'That looks like our entire stock of heroin,' said Stenson.

'Yes. Can you value it for us?'

'Ten pounds an ounce.'

'H'm. A tidy tickle. And you could multiply the value by twenty, or fifty, if a snuff pedlar got hold of it.'

'That's right,' Stenson agreed. 'It depends how much they adulterate it.'

16

'None of this stuff is any good for fingerprints,' said Martineau. 'If we had made an arrest, we'd have had to take it along as evidence. As things are, we don't need it at the moment. Can you put it on one side and keep it available if needed?'

'I can do that, box and all,' said Stenson. 'I don't think we have any of the stuff going out in the near future. Would it matter if I brought it to court two or three packets short?'

'No, that could be explained. What about this rubber band? Does it belong to the firm?'

Stenson shook his head. 'That's a round of inner tube from an awful big tyre,' he said. 'I've never seen anything like that about the place.'

Martineau picked up the rubber band, folded it carefully, and pocketed it. Devery got a receipt for the heroin from Stenson, who was obviously getting ready to ask Martineau for the full story.

Then the sergeant was seen to smother a yawn and look at his watch. 'Yes,' said Martineau. 'There's nothing more for you to do here. I'll want your report—and yours—er—Policewoman—as soon as possible tomorrow, but now you can go and get some sleep. Drive your partner home before you take the car in, Devery.'

'Yes, sir.' Devery and Rosamund allowed the watchman to take them to the front door. They stood on the doorstep for a moment, breathing the cool night air.

'You needn't bother driving me home,' said Rosamund.

'Orders,' Devery replied.

They went along to the Jaguar, which was still standing in front of a loading bay. Devery took the wheel. During the uneventful afternoon Rosamund had told him that she lived with her parents in the suburb of Shirwell. He began to drive in that direction.

'Does your mother worry?' he asked.

'Not particularly. I told her C.I.D. work was uncertain. Late hours and that.'

'*Will* she worry when she finds you've been in the wars?'

'She won't know. She'll be in bed, and tomorrow I'll wear something different. By the time she finds out, if she ever does, it'll be past history. Something to laugh about.'

'You're sure you're all right?' Devery asked. Actually he was thinking about another young woman, who had been expecting to hear from him that evening.

'Yes, quite sure,' Rosamund replied.

'I saw you tackle that fellow. You're a brave girl.'

'Tut-tut. I was honly a-doing hof me duty, zurr.'

'An echo or something led me wrong. When they crashed the van into the police car I chased them back into the building. They went through a door and barred it against me, and not knowing my way around I was flummoxed. They seemed to be heading in the direction of you and your coal chute, so I ran back the way I'd come. When I got outside I heard a window go, and, as I say, the high buildings or something gave me a wrong impression of where it was.'

'I can understand that. When the A.P. car got it, I thought it was ours.'

'Yes. Well, I ran the wrong way, the long way round. If I'd gone the other way I would have intercepted the fellow you tackled.'

'It's the luck of the game.'

'That's just it. I'm usually lucky. I'm not used to having my plans go wrong. It worries me when they do.'

'Never mind. You recovered the goods.'

'Ah, but I made a hash of it,' said Devery with a touch of bitterness. He was thinking, vengefully, that the character in the white mask had not seen the last of him. He would see to it that the fellow didn't give him the dummy a second time. He would teach him not to throw lady coppers about, too.

He could have said all that to the girl, but he would have felt as if he were talking like a blowhard. She sensed that he could have said more. He would be wanting to have another go. He was big and strong, but not so heavy as the man in the white mask. He was younger probably, and more agile. It would be a good match, but she did not want to see it.

They drove on in silence, and Devery dwelt once more upon the matter of the girl who had been expecting to hear from him. Her name was Ella Bowie, and she worked at the Northland Hotel. Since he had not been able to get to the hotel to see her, he ought to have found time to telephone. She would be wondering why he had not done so. She had no telephone at home, and it was too late now to go and see her. Saturday tomorrow, Ella's busy day. He decided that he would try to see her tomorrow.

Ella would still be assuming that he had spent the day prowling with the homely Ducklin. It would be a good thing for her peace of mind if she could go on thinking that. She would get into a rare state if she knew that her love was spending his working days with an unusually good-looking girl. Good-looking? Policewoman Valentine was beautiful. There was no doubt about it. If Ella got a good look at this girl she would be sick with jealousy, and all the protestations in the world would not make any difference.

Devery reflected that he would have to be very circumspect, and keep Ella in ignorance of P.W. Valentine's existence. He would keep her in ignorance as long as he could, at any rate. He did not feel optimistic about that. His experience of his colleagues made him gloomily afraid that Ella would be told about Miss Valentine. Some horrible detective officer would wander into the Northland and enjoy giving Ella the facts, highly coloured. Yes, some dirty dog would do that. There were just a few men in the C.I.D. who suspected that he was unduly friendly with Ella, though none of them knew enough to be certain.

# THREE

THE duty of writing the preliminary Crime Report on the B.M. break-in was the task of Devery, the first policeman on the scene. Rosamund's contribution to the file was in the form of a statement. She had a typewriter and some official stationery at home, and she was able to do the work in the peaceful atmosphere of her room. She went on duty at two o'clock with the statement completed, and when she met Devery she was not surprised to learn that he had been down in the morning and written the report and his own statement.

'I thought Martineau might have something for me to do,' he explained.

'And had he?'

'No. He told me to go away. He hadn't a thing to do except look for likely clients in the files. He gets a bit tetchy when his affairs are that way.'

They got the Jaguar and started their patrol. Devery continued Rosamund's education. Held up in traffic in Lacy Street he said: 'See that rat-faced fellow in the green hat, walking as if he's on broken glass? That's Hammer Toe Hobson, sneak-in man.' When the car was held up momentarily in Holland Street he said: 'Take a good look at this swarthy character coming along. The man with the furrowed cheeks and the hand-painted tie. That's Georgie Vane, suspected of living on the immoral earnings of several girls.' In All Saints Road he said: 'Get the white Rolls? The man just getting out of it is Dixie Costello. He lives over that restaurant.'

'So *that's* Dixie Costello,' Rosamund said. 'Who's the girl?'

20

'Popsie,' replied Devery. 'He always calls them Popsie.'

The afternoon wore on, a fine afternoon for the thousands of shoppers in the heart of the city. The sergeant and the policewoman saw no pickpocket or bag-snatcher at work, no 'wanted' man or woman, nothing to break the monotony of their endless cruising. They talked over the events of the previous night. It was a profitless discussion. The thieves had left nothing by which they could be traced. The rubber band in Martineau's possession bore no identifiable fingerprints. The damaged three-tonner yielded only the fingerprints of the regular driver, though there had been no time for it to be 'wiped over' after the collision with the A.P. car. Obviously the thieves had worn gloves. The absence of 'dabs' made a fact of a matter about which eye-witnesses could not be certain.

At half past five Devery said: 'We'd better go and have some tea. On the way, stop at the first phone-box you see. I've a call to make.'

Rosamund stopped the car beside an unoccupied telephone kiosk, and the sergeant made his call.

'Hello, darling,' Ella said. 'What happened to you last night?'

'I was busy, Ella. I didn't phone you because things were so quiet I expected to be standing at your bar before you closed. Then just as I was getting ready to wrap up, a job came in. A break-in at the British Medicaments warehouse in Arundel Street. I was kept there pretty late. Ruined my blue suit, too.'

'Oh dear. What happened?'

'I chased a man and fell over my own feet.'

'Were you hurt, darling?'

'No. Only mortified. I'll see you tonight, eh? The job isn't moving at all. I shall be off at ten.'

'It's Saturday, remember. There's sure to be something. If you can't get here, come along to my place later.'

'Even if I'm very late?'

'Come as late as you like, but come. I'll have something for your supper. I may have something to tell you too.'

'Some information?'

'Sort of. Something I've been noticing. I'm not going to tell you over the phone. I want to be sure I see you tonight.'

'I'll be there, my dear. Never fear.'

Devery went back to the car. That was typical of Ella, he thought. She had something for him, and she was using it as an extra inducement to get him to her house. He wondered how long his more-or-less secret affair with her would go on. Both of them knew that it would have to come to an end sometime. The inevitable parting was something which they never discussed. Ella was 'unsuitable'. She was not merely unsuitable because she was a barmaid of high sexual voltage who had been, and still was, the target of many amorous advances. She was a woman who had made herself into a widow. The husband she had killed—a clear case of self-defence—had been a notorious criminal. *That* was the shadow from her past which a police authority would never forget. Any policeman who married Ella Bowie could write off all his prospects of promotion.

Devery was ambitious. Ella understood that quite well. She did not expect him to marry her. She dreaded the day when he would meet some girl he would want to marry, but she never mentioned it.

At least, Devery thought, nobody had yet told Ella about the new order concerning prowlers. She still thought that her lover was spending his time with a fellow detective. That was something to be thankful for.

He and Rosamund went to the police canteen. He had beans on toast at a table with two sergeants. The girl joined a group of policewomen and had beans on toast too. After the forty-five minutes' break she went out to the car. Devery looked into the C.I.D. before he met her there.

'Nothing new down the mine,' he reported, as he took the wheel. 'Martineau is still doing it the hard way.'

Though it was Saturday night, they toured without interruption until nine o'clock. At that time they were in Highfield, a suburb of semi-detached modern houses owned

22

and lived in by people with settled occupations. Martineau himself lived in Highfield, and his nearest neighbours were a bank clerk, a solicitor's clerk, a commercial traveller and a schoolmaster.

Devery had just pointed out Martineau's house to his companion when the radio growled: 'Have we got anybody in Highfield?'

Rosamund answered at once: 'Sergeant Devery and Policewoman Valentine in Highfield Road.'

'Go to two-o-two Edgley Crescent,' the Headquarters man said. 'Naylor is the name. Miss Muriel Naylor. It's a crime. Alleged housebreaking, alleged rape. Reported by a Dr. Lindsay on nine-nine-nine.'

Rosamund was caught professionally off guard. She gasped: 'Did you say rape?'

'I said rape,' the man replied flatly.

Without a word Devery turned the car in the direction of Edgley Crescent. He was thinking of the grin on the face of the operator at Headquarters. He was just as sure of that grin as if he had seen it. The word would be passed around, with sniggers. Devery and his girl friend had gone to a rape job. *Miss* Muriel Naylor. Maybe a girl of fifteen, nearly insane with shame and horror. But because Policewoman Valentine was something to make their eyes pop, it was all very funny. Why, he demanded silently, did he have to be the first detective sergeant to be saddled with a woman? And such an essentially feminine one! Why hadn't they given him somebody like Policewoman Sergeant O'Keefe? The O'Keefe was nobody's laughing matter.

Could he have read Rosamund's thoughts he would have been surprised. She was reflecting that this was suitable work for a policewoman. For getting a coherent statement from an outraged girl, surely a woman would be better than a big-footed policeman.

'I may be able to help you with the injured party,' she said.

'Sure,' Devery replied shortly. 'All girls together.'

'Was that remark necessary?'

'Sorry.'

'Are you thinking about titters behind the hand at Headquarters?'

'Such a thing did cross my mind. Forget it.'

'You think *I* care about those leering apes? Don't tell me to forget it, Sergeant.'

Devery was silent, deservedly rebuked. They were in Edgley Crescent, and Rosamund turned the car's moveable spotlight on to the houses. 'Here it is,' she said. Devery stopped the car behind a frog-mouthed Citroen which was already there.

Rosamund followed him to the front door of No. 202, but when he stopped there she went on to the back. She stopped in a position where she could see the back door, and yet be seen by Devery.

He rang the bell. Almost immediately the door was opened by a neatly dressed, compact, quick-looking man about forty years of age. 'Are you the police?' he asked.

'Detective Sergeant Devery. Who are you?'

'Lindsay is the name,' the man said in the moderate accent of the educated Scot. 'I'm Miss Naylor's doctor.'

'Is the place clear? Has the assailant gone?'

The doctor showed surprise. 'I presume he has. He could be miles away by now.'

'Just one thing while we're alone, Doctor. Was it actually rape, or just an attempt?'

'It was rape, without a doubt. Also, without a doubt, it was defloration. The signs are unusually clear.'

'Thanks,' said Devery. He called up Rosamund, and introduced her.

'A policewoman,' the doctor said. 'A very good idea.'

'Go with the doctor and see Miss Naylor,' Devery said. 'I'll take a quick look around out here.'

Rosamund followed the doctor into the house, and she took a good look at things as she went along, as almost every woman does. The place was nicely and sensibly furnished. The furniture was far from being new, but it did not seem to have had a great deal of use. Even the

24

comfortable living-room had a little-used look. It was the home of a person who lived alone.

There were two pictures in the living-room. They looked like coloured enlargements: the Castle of Chillon with intensely blue sky and water, and an intensely blue-and-white view of the Matterhorn. There was a bookcase with books which had been used. On a little coffee-table beside the fireplace there was a tray, with tea-things and biscuits. This was the home of a woman who had always lived alone: a woman no longer very young.

Surprisingly, on the sideboard, there was a bottle of sherry and two glasses.

Lindsay returned to the little hallway and stood at the foot of the stairs. 'Miss Naylor,' he called. 'The police are here.'

'All right,' a woman replied in a voice which, in the circumstances, had an astonishing strength and calmness. 'I don't want them up here. I'll be down in a minute.'

The doctor went back to Rosamund. 'She's taking it extremely well,' he said. 'It *is* rape, you know. Is there anything I can tell you while we're waiting for her?'

'Obviously you've examined her,' said Rosamund, put at ease by his assumption of her professional detachment.

'Yes. At first she wanted to keep the matter completely confidential, but I pointed out the danger to other lonely ladies. A maniac of this type wants locking up, and quickly. She accepted that immediately. I told her that a police surgeon would want to examine her and she didn't like it at all. She insisted that I examine her before I called the police. She hoped the police surgeon would take my word for it, and waive his own examination.'

'The delay in calling the police will have allowed the man to get clear away.'

'I realized that at the time. But with a woman who has just had an experience of that kind——'

'Yes, of course. There would be danger of hysteria. She'll be in a shocked condition.'

'Not as bad as you'd expect. Naturally, I took the medical

precautions necessary after a happening of that sort. We don't want any physical consequences, do we?'

Rosamund was sickened by the thought, but she stiffened her chin. 'Certainly not,' she answered crisply.

'It's very odd,' the doctor went on, obviously interested beyond professional requirements. 'According to Miss Naylor there were two men in the house, but she only saw one of them. The other one kept out of sight.'

There were footsteps on the stairs, and then a woman walked into the room. She was a big woman of excellent proportions, in age approaching forty. While she could not be called handsome, neither could she be called plain. Rosamund thought she had never seen a more open-faced woman. The wide blue eyes showed considerable intelligence but no cunning. She gazed at the girl in surprise.

'This is a policewoman, Muriel,' the doctor said.

Miss Naylor's surprise did not diminish. 'Have they sent you here alone?' she wanted to know.

Smiling, Rosamund shook her head. The question was typical of an essentially 'good' person, she thought. She had her own private definitions of good and bad people, irrespective of police records. Bad people were bad-tempered. They had to be considered, and their likes and dislikes allowed for, though they considered only themselves. They would say what they liked, but you had to be careful what you said to them. They would ruin your day with gratuitous insolence, which they called plain speaking, and go on their way without another thought about you. Oh, she could go on all day about bad people. Many of them had personal charm which they could switch on and off like electricity. Many of them were regarded as 'characters' whose behaviour should be tolerated. Rosamund tolerated them when she had to, which was when she could not avoid them. She preferred good people even if they were sometimes rather dull. This Miss Naylor was obviously a good person. Her first thought, after a dreadful experience, was for another woman who appeared to have been sent alone on an unpleasant mission.

Devery could be heard entering the house. He came into the living-room, and was introduced.

'I think perhaps I should go now,' Lindsay said with an interrogative glance at the sergeant. He received a nod in reply; his statement could be taken later. Smiling, he reached for Miss Naylor's wrist and held the pulse for a little while. 'You'll be all right, but I'll look in tomorrow,' he said, then he picked up his bag.

As he departed a look of desolation passed over his patient's candid face, as visible as a riffle of wind on smooth water. It was gone in a moment, and she turned rather blankly to the two police officers. 'Er, would you like a drink?' she asked.

Without a change of expression Devery thanked her and declined the offer. 'Do you feel that you need something?' he asked.

'No, I've had something,' she replied. She looked round absently. He perceived her requirement and brought out his cigarettes. When they were seated, and smoking, he asked: 'Would you like me to go away while you tell your story to Policewoman Valentine, or is it all right if I stay?'

Miss Naylor thought about that. 'I think you'd better hear it,' she said.

'Very well. Would you please tell it from the beginning?'

A brief apologetic smile came and went. 'It was so simple it sounds silly. I don't know what time it was exactly. Round about eight-thirty, I think. I had been watching the television, and I decided to have my bit of supper and read in bed. I went into the kitchen and put the kettle on, then I went upstairs and got undressed, and put on my dressing-gown, just as I am now. I came down, brewed the tea, and carried the tray in here. I'd just poured myself a cup and sat down by the fire when I heard something at the back door. A sort of light knock, just once. Well, I wasn't sure, and I was waiting for whoever it was to knock again when the kitchen door opened and this man walked into the room. I don't know how he got in. The back door was locked.'

27

'Did you leave the light on in the kitchen when you went upstairs?'

'Yes. I was only a minute or two.'

'It's a mortise lock. The man looked into the keyhole and saw that the key was in the lock. He prepared some sticky paper while you were making the tea. He stuck the paper on the glass panel near the lock, and knocked the panel in. Then he pulled away the paper and the broken glass with it. After that he had only to reach through and turn the key.'

'Oh dear. I shouldn't have left the key in the lock.'

'Never mind. Go on with your story.'

'Well, as I say, he walked in, a great big man with his right hand down at his side, holding something out of sight. I said: "How did you get in? What do you want?"'

'He said: "I want you to keep quiet, for a start. Just keep quiet, then you'll be all right. If you *don't* keep quiet I'll have to cut you short with this." Then he showed me an open razor in his hand. He grinned at me and said: "It's as sharp as a razor." Ooh, it looked horrible! I stared at it like a mesmerized rabbit. When I looked at him I saw that his eyes were sort of glittering, but he was quite calm. I thought he was just going to keep me sitting there while he ransacked the house.'

'You say his eyes glittered? Did you smell liquor?'

'Not then. I did later. But I wouldn't say he was under the influence.'

'What about drugs? Would you say he'd been taking drugs?'

'I don't know. I've never seen anybody who's been taking drugs. As I say, he was quite calm, and I suppose I kept calm myself because it all happened so simply I could hardly believe it. I had that helpless feeling you have in a horrible dream.'

Miss Naylor looked at Rosamund, as if she imagined that that young woman would have had a similar experience, and would understand. The policewoman's pencil was flying across a page of her official pocket-book, but the pause made her look up and nod in sympathy.

Miss Naylor went on: 'I heard something in the kitchen then. It was quite a definite noise of somebody opening and shutting a cupboard door. The man took no notice, and I guessed that there were two of them. He made me go upstairs, and he walked right behind me. Then he told me to lie on my bed, and I refused. He showed his teeth then, and his razor. He said I could lie down as I was, or with my throat sliced open.'

'Were those his exact words?'

'Yes. "Sliced open" was what he said.' The woman shuddered. 'Then—well, it happened. Oh dear.'

'And afterwards?'

'He—he gave me a hearty slap, and said: "Good girl." He told me to stay where I was, and he went downstairs. I thought I'd seen the last of him, and I was waiting to hear them both go, but after a few minutes he came back with a glass of sherry. He gave it to me as if it were a Christmas present or something—really, my own sherry! —and stood watching me drink it. He was actually smiling, quite pleased with himself. Then the other man called him, and he said: "Good night, lady " and went running down the stairs. I heard them go out of the back door, then I came down and phoned Dr. Lindsay.'

'Has anything been stolen?'

Miss Naylor appeared to be slightly astonished. She stared round the room, and then her glance sharpened and focused on a brown pigskin handbag which lay on the sideboard. Devery got up and crossed the room to pick up the bag, noting that it was not of a texture which would hold a fingerprint. He handed it to its owner.

She opened the bag and took out a purse. 'This is the only money I have in the house,' she said as she opened the purse. Then: 'They've taken my money! Eight pounds in notes they've taken, and left the change! Well, they *are* mean!'

Rosamund was startled, and Devery repressed a smile.

'After drinking most of your sherry, too,' he said, looking. at the bottle.

'I don't have liquor. I just keep a bottle of sherry in, in case somebody calls,' she explained naively.

'Don't touch the bottle or the glasses,' the sergeant warned. 'If you don't mind, I'll go and take a look upstairs.

She nodded, and he went. She looked at Rosamund, at her left hand holding the notebook.

'You're not married, are you?' she remarked. 'You're not missing anything. I'm surprised I didn't faint, but I'm glad I didn't. I wouldn't have known what it was like, would I? Believe it or not, it was the first time for me. And I didn't speak more than half a dozen words to the man.'

'How do you feel now?' Rosamund asked, with womanly concern.

Miss Naylor considered how she felt. 'Not as bad as you'd think,' she said with surprise in her voice. 'Dr. Lindsay assured me I'll be all right. No babies, or anything. But it wouldn't be so bad having a baby the Married Women's Union couldn't blame you for, would it? I wouldn't terribly mind a baby, you know. I've never had anything to do with my money except save it, and I could afford to bring up a child.'

Rosamund reflected that Miss Naylor should have been a good man's wife and the mother of stalwart sons. It was a shame, she thought, that such a woman had to go through life without a mate. She uttered the only remark she could think of in the circumstances. 'You'll be perfectly all right.'

Devery returned, balancing an empty wineglass on the palm of his hand. He placed it carefully on the sideboard with the others.

'There'll be a little more bother for you yet, Miss Naylor,' he said. 'The fingerprint men had better go over this place first thing in the morning. Until then I want you to touch as little as possible in the house. I'll have them here soon after nine o'clock. Will that be all right?'

'Yes. I'm always up by nine on a Sunday.'

30

'Well, I should be getting a description of your attacker on the air, though I suppose he'll be far from here now. You say he was a big man?'

'Yes, a big handsome brute. Not fat. Nice broad shoulders. A proper man, really.'

'Fair or dark?'

'Dark. Swarthy, almost. Dark-brown eyes. No moustache or anything, but he seemed to have nice teeth. His hair was really lovely, black and glossy and wavy. Oh dear, I seem to be recommending him for something, don't I. The horrid beast. All the same, I bet lots of women have been raped by worse-looking men.'

'What age would you say he was?'

'Oh, about thirty-five.'

'How was he dressed?'

'Dark suit and white shirt. Black shoes, I think. Black-and-blue tie with a small diamond pattern.'

'Do you know if he had a hat?'

'I never saw a hat. He was bare-headed all the time.'

'Any peculiarities? A limp? A way of walking? Marks or scars?'

'I didn't notice anything like that.'

'What about his voice?'

'Rather deep. Sort of baritone.'

'Could you place his accent?'

Miss Naylor thought about that. 'I'm afraid I can't help you much there,' she said. 'It wasn't a gentleman's accent either, come to think of it. He sounded a bit like the commissionaire at the works, sort of synthetic. That's it exactly! You know, when a man—not an officer—has been in the Army or the Navy for years and years, and has been to Singapore and Khartoum and Bangalore and all those places, he gets a sort of accent which makes his own hard to identify. This man could have been a Yorkshireman or an Ulsterman or a Cornishman or anything like that.'

'But not a Kentishman or a Cockney?'

'No, definitely not.'

31

'And you think he's an old soldier?'

'No, I don't. I think he's a man who hasn't spent his life in one place, like I have.'

'I see. What is your occupation, Miss Naylor?'

'I'm a secretary. I'm secretary to Mr. Lyle, the managing director of British Medicaments.'

Devery was suddenly very still. Rosamund's pencil was lifted from the paper. She looked wide-eyed at Miss Naylor.

'What's the matter?' the lady asked.

'Do you have a key to the place?'

'For the office door. And for Mr. Lyle's office. Oh! That burglary last night! Is there some connection?'

'Where are your keys?'

The woman opened her handbag and searched among its contents with increasing agitation. Failing to find what she sought, she rose to her feet and upturned the bag on the living-room table. She spread out the jumble of personal accessories with a large clean hand, then she felt around the lining of the bag. 'They're gone,' she said tragically. 'My keys are gone.'

Without a word Devery went to the telephone, which was on a table near the foot of the stairs. He dialled nine-nine-nine, and in a moment was giving his message in clear measured tones: 'Sergeant Devery speaking from Highfield. I have reason to believe that thieves involved in the housebreaking and rape at Edgley Crescent have got possession of the key to the office door of British Medicaments in Arundel Street. They may have staged this job simply to get the key, and they may be on the premises at B.M. at this very moment. I'll hold the line while you put the word out, then I'll give you a description of a suspect.'

He waited a short while, then he gave the description of Miss Naylor's 'big handsome brute' to Headquarters. He returned to the living-room to face an indignant woman.

'It's shameful,' she declared. 'To think they did that to me, just to get my office key! Couldn't they have simply taken it?'

Since Miss Naylor had perceived the humiliating truth, there was no point in trying to disguise it:

'They didn't want you to know that they were seeking the key,' Devery explained. 'If you hadn't happened to mention your place of work, the loss of the key wouldn't have been discovered until tomorrow or Monday.'

# FOUR

When they left Miss Naylor, Devery and Rosamund drove to Arundel Street. The scene outside the offices of British Medicaments Limited was not typical of the aftermath of a major crime. On Saturday night in the commercial district there were not many people about, and consequently there were no bystanders. Neither were there any reporters. The uniformed constable on duty at the door had no one to keep him company.

The P.C. stopped Rosamund. Devery was speaking to the man about this when she produced her warrant card and settled the matter. They went into the main office, where Martineau was the centre of activities. His thoughtful frown did not change when he saw Devery. 'Your tip came too late,' he said.

'Sorry about that, sir. Did they get clear away with the stuff?'

'They did.' The frown became a mirthless grin. 'They got all the stuff I left in the manager's care last night, and in addition they took a consignment of cocaine hydro-chloride.'

'Is that any different from ordinary cocaine?'

'I don't know. I expect it'll be a narcotic, or they wouldn't have taken it.'

'Well, well. Is that ten pounds an ounce, too?'

'Something like that, I imagine. They didn't give the watchman time to dial nine-nine-nine this time. They came in quietly and caught him unaware. They locked him in the storeroom again, then picked up the stuff and scarpered.'

'The same men?'

34

'He thinks so. They had their faces covered. He only saw two of them, same as last night.'

'They were determined to get the stuff, weren't they?'

'Yes. I have an idea about that.' Martineau pulled a folded newspaper from his pocket and opened it. 'This morning's paper,' he said. 'This article made me smile a smile of pleasure. It shouldn't have done. It should have warned me.'

Devery looked where the big forefinger was pointing, and read a brief article about the seizure by Customs officers at London Docks of a large consignment of smuggled heroin.

'From Istanbul,' Devery commented.

'*Via* Istanbul, at any rate. You get the picture? These people are regular suppliers of narcotics to some market or other. They guarantee delivery, apparently. And in case anything goes wrong, they have places like British Medicaments on their list, with ready-made plans for getting in.'

'They knew last night about the seizure of heroin.'

'Of course. Somebody would phone them from London within the hour. So they got ready to tickle this place. I'm assuming they already had their plan to get Miss Naylor's keys, but that was for to-night. Last night, when they were giving the joint a preliminary case, they found they could get down a coal chute. So they gave it a try. It didn't come off, so to-night they fell back on the original plan, and that did come off.'

'There's one thing seems odd. They covered their faces when they cracked this place, both times. But that character at Miss Naylor's didn't cover his face. *She'll* know him again.'

'Yes, that is a bit queer. We might get the reason for it later, if there is a reason. You know how crooks are, meticulous one minute and careless as hell the next. Anyway, Miss Naylor can have the pleasure of looking through the picture books for her client. Will she make a good witness, do you think?'

MAURICE PROCTER

'I'd say so. She seems to tell the truth and nothing but.
No embroidery, as far as I can see.'

'Fine,' said Martineau. He gazed at a man who was
busily dusting the storeroom door for fingerprints. 'It
looks as if we're still going to have to find something in
the records. Miss Naylor should be a big help.'

'Anything we can do for you here, sir?'

'No.' Martineau looked at his watch. 'You might as well
go home. Let this young woman get some beauty sleep.
You never know, we might keep her very busy later on.
Good night, both of you.'

Devery drove towards Headquarters. He and Rosamund
had spent more than an hour at Edgley Crescent, and now
the time was twenty minutes to eleven. People were
leaving places of entertainment and making their ways
home, or in search of supper. It was a time to drive slowly,
because there were many people about and some of them
were in a state of Saturday-night exuberance. This applied
to both drivers and pedestrians. Devery did not hurry. He
did not want to involve the precious Jaguar in an accident.

In Lacy Street the crowds strolled. There was no cold
wind to make them nip along, no rain to make the women
fear for their clothes, hats and hair-dos. A fine, mild night
like this was to be enjoyed. The brilliantly lighted shop
windows invited strollers to linger, the twinkling, shifting
electric signs beckoned for their attention, the traffic only
demanded that people should keep out of its way.

To Devery the policeman even a small crowd at the kerb
was more noticeable than the biggest neon sign in the
street. There was the crowd, and an old blue Triumph
car. He pulled in to the kerb before he reached the Triumph,
but remained in his seat, waiting until he had seen what
was going on.

At first there appeared to be nothing happening; nothing
which should have drawn even a small crowd. The bonnet
cover on the offside of the car had been opened, and two
men were stooping over the engine. Then Devery corrected
that first impression. One man was stooping over the engine

36

and the other man was leaning on the radiator cover, offering advice. The crowd seemed to regard this as a form of entertainment.

Devery moved the Jaguar a little nearer to the Triumph. This operation was observed, and ignored, by the man who was acting as adviser. Devery lowered the window beside him, and leaned out to listen.

'Tell you what, Herbie,' the adviser was saying. 'Take the swizzle pins outa the gudgeon box an' give 'em a slick of oil. Tha' should make it start.'

'Am tickling 'er,' Herbie replied solemnly. 'This ole girl likes tickling.'

'They all like it,' the adviser rejoined. He was resting his chin on his hand, and his elbow was on the shiny top of the radiator. The elbow slipped, and the crowd laughed.

'A bit of clowning going on here,' Devery murmured to Rosamund. 'These two fellows may be drunk.'

The adviser smiled vacantly at the bystanders, then he appeared to ignore them. 'Why don't you fasten the snaffle to the cylinder head?' he wanted to know. 'Then all you have to do is tighten up the martingale and we're off.'

'Shurrup,' said Herbie amiably. 'I'm the man who's making her go.'

'Next Chris'mus, happen,' came the retort, and the crowd snickered.

A dark blue helmet appeared above the heads of the crowd. A voice said clearly: 'Come along now! Pass along, *please*! Don't block the street.'

People moved reluctantly. The newcomer, a tall young constable, kept them on the move like a herdsman. He 'saw them off', then returned to the Triumph. The beginnings of a new crowd immediately formed behind him.

The man who had been leaning on the radiator stood upright. Devery noted that he was a big man, wearing a dark suit, black shoes, white shirt, dark tie, and a grey trilby which was pushed to the back of his head. He was about thirty-five years old. He had dark hair and eyes, and he was handsome.

A muffled exclamation came from Rosamund, but the sergeant said: 'No, I don't think so. He wouldn't be acting the fool like this if he'd just done the B.M. job.'

The big man was grinning at the constable. He was swaying slightly. 'We're in the guinea ring now,' he said thickly. 'Distinguished audience.'

A few people tittered. The P.C. did not like that very much. 'What's the matter?' he asked. 'Can't you get her to start?'

The big man raised his eyebrows and shrugged elaborately. 'Is it not obvious?' he asked of the world at large. 'Is it not obvious to any person of intelligence?'

The constable liked that even less. He walked round the car and looked at the engine. Then he looked inside the car. 'It might be a good idea if you switched on,' he said drily.

The man called Herbie stood erect, tottered, and put a hand on the car to steady himself. When he saw that, Devery muttered: 'You stay here.' He got out of the Jaguar and went to join the group beside the Triumph. Herbie and the big man observed his arrival with drunken impassiveness. The P.C. turned to see what they were looking at, and said: 'Hello, Sarge. Glad to see you. These two look as if they've had a few.'

Devery wanted to know who the men were, and one sure way of finding out was to get them into a police station. 'They seem to have had more than a few,' he said. 'I'll stay with you. Get on with it.'

The P.C. nodded. 'Which of you two is the driver of the car?' he asked.

'I am,' said Herbie.

'I am,' said the big man.

'We both are,' said Herbie.

'Who *owns* the car?' the P.C. demanded.

'I do,' said the big man.

'I do,' said Herbie.

'We both own it,' Herbie explained.

'Which of you is supposed to be in charge of it at this moment?' the P.C. wanted to know.

'We both are,' said Herbie.

The P.C. turned his head aside. 'Think they're good enough?' he murmured to Devery.

'One of them is,' the sergeant replied. 'Find out which one, and the other can come along for the ride. I'll support you. Even if the doctor gives them the verdict, there'll be no harm done.'

'Which of you holds the log-book for this car?' the P.C. asked.

'Neither of us. It's at home,' the big man said.

'Which of you licensed it?'

'Both of us. It's a joint affair.'

The policeman paused, temporarily at a loss. Devery knew what to do, but he remained silent. He wanted to see how his colleague would handle it.

The P.C. showed that he was a man who would not be baulked by a technicality. 'You're drunk,' he said bluntly to Herbie.

Herbie appeared to take that as an insult. He drew himself to his full height, let go of the car, and had to grab it again. 'I'm as sober as seven Sundays,' he said with dignity, and his pronunciation of the phrase left the bystanders in no doubt that he was a Welshman.

The big man jostled Herbie as he came forward. 'My friend is *not* drunk,' he declared. He put a hand on the constable's shoulder, apparently to steady himself.

The P.C. knocked the hand away. 'You're drunk, too. What's your name?'

'Gabriel Lovell is my name, and I don't care who knows, it.'

'All right. You both claim to be in charge of the car, so you both can come with me. We'll sort this out at the police station. Go on, get in the car!'

Devery held open the offside rear door, and Gabriel, about six feet one, and Herbie, about two inches shorter, allowed the P.C. to bundle them into the back of the car.

'You're making a big mistake,' Herbie threatened. 'I'll have your coat off your back for this.'

'Monday morning you'll be sorry,' Gabriel said with an air of satisfaction. 'Monday morning when the beak hears about thish—this truly dishgrasheful affair, you've had it.'

The young policeman had heard that sort of talk before, and never been in danger of losing his uniform. He put down the bonnet cover and secured it, then he walked round the car and took the seat beside the driver's. Devery slipped in behind the wheel and switched on. The car would not start.

'Ha ha!' Herbie chortled. 'We'll be here all night. Make yourself comfortable, Gabe.'

'She's flooded,' the P.C. muttered.

Devery nodded, and tried again. The starter whirred and the engine caught. It roared, coughed, and settled down. Devery drove to Headquarters, and Rosamund followed in the Jaguar.

In the charge-room of 'A' Division, the P.C., whose name was Armstrong, explained his dilemma to a sergeant. The duty inspector came to listen, and frown at the prisoners. 'Get the doctor,' he said to the sergeant.

Instructed by Devery, Rosamund went along to the C.I.D., where there were some soundproof telephone boxes. She looked up the number of British Medicaments, and dialled. Martineau himself answered the call.

'Policewoman Valentine, sir,' the girl said.

'I thought I told you to go home to bed,' the chief inspector retorted. 'Does this mean you've gone and walked into another spot of bother?'

'Yes, sir, but it isn't exactly mine. There are two men here. They've been picked up for drunk in charge, but it looks like a borderline job. Sergeant Devery suggests that you ought to have a look at them before they're allowed to go home.'

'Why?'

'One of them answers the description we got from Miss Naylor.'

'I see. Right. I'm on my way.'

Rosamund returned to the charge-room in time to see

Gabriel Lovell walk quite steadily with arm outstretched towards a spot on the wall, and place the tip of his forefinger exactly on it. When he had done that he walked with equal steadiness along a white line, explaining as he did so that he could always do tightrope-walking better without a rope. Meanwhile, at the charge-room counter, Herbert, surnamed Small, counted pennies, shillings, halfpennies sixpences, florins and half-crowns with the deftness of a bank clerk.

Witnessing these actions, the duty inspector gave P.C. Armstrong a very black look indeed, and the young man turned red. Devery saw the look. He drew the inspector aside and explained something to him. The inspector nodded, looked at Armstrong again, and nodded to him also. The constable's face cleared. Devery was supporting him as he had said he would.

The divisional police surgeon arrived, not surprised to be called out on a Saturday night, but not pleased about it, either. He also frowned at the prisoners. 'Have they asked for their own doctor?' he wanted to know.

'They were given the opportunity to call a doctor,' the inspector replied. 'They didn't want one.'

'We rely on your professional probity, Doctor,' said Lovell blandly.

'H'm.' The surgeon was not impressed. 'Will you submit to the urine test?' he asked.

'Certainly. Anything you say, Doctor. Breathalizer as well, if you like.'

The doctor made his tests. At the end he looked up angrily. 'Who said these men were drunk?'

P.C. Armstrong had been expecting that. 'I did, sir,' he said.

'I was with the constable,' said Devery. 'I also thought they were drunk. They acted drunk.'

'Ah,' said the doctor. 'Well, I'm going home. You can do what you like with them, but they're not drunk. They weren't drunk an hour ago, either.'

Martineau walked in as the doctor walked out. 'What's

41

bitten him?' he asked, his gaze already fixed on the prisoners.

'These two brought in drunk, only they're not,' the inspector explained. He turned to the two men and spoke with soft menace: 'Had your little joke, did you? Thought you'd take the mickey out of a policeman?'

Herbie was earnest. 'Nothing like that, sir. I *told* him I wasn't drunk. Of course I'll admit I've had a drink or *two*.'

'It isn't my idea of fun, playing games with policemen,' said Gabriel Lovell soberly. '*I* didn't get myself arrested on purpose, I can assure you.'

Devery stepped forward and confronted Gabriel. 'You can't assure me of anything,' he said. 'I watched your little game from the start, and before you get away from here I'm going to know something about you. To start with, where is your home?'

The man smiled. 'Wherever I happen to be.'

'No fixed abode, eh? Well, where did it use to be?'

'As I told you, wherever it happened to be.'

'You mean you never had a home?'

'I always had a home, and it always went with me. I'm a gypsy.'

'A real gypsy, or just here today and gone tomorrow?'

'I have nothing but gypsy blood in my veins.'

'Where's your caravan?'

'Boyton.'

'Dodge City?'

'Yes.'

'How long has it been there?'

'About three weeks.'

'Got a wife and children living in it?'

'No. I'm not married.'

'How do you make a living?'

'Various ways. I can turn my hand to anything, gypsy fashion.'

'Such as?'

'Well, trading for one thing.'

'It used to be horse trading, didn't it? There'll be none of that these days.'

'You're wrong, you know. I've broken and sold ponies in the past twelvemonth. I have also dealt in second-hand cars. That's the modern version of horse trading.'

'All right.' Devery turned and looked at Martineau. The chief inspector nodded. Devery asked: 'Where were you between eight and nine o'clock to-night?'

'I was giving a lecture.'

'You were what?'

'I was giving a lecture to the Literary and Philosophical Society, at their rooms.'

'What were you lecturing about?'

'The title of my paper was "The Gypsy in Modern Times".'

'The Lit and Phil don't have dealings with people like you.'

Gabriel smiled. 'They did on this occasion.'

Baffled, Devery swung to face Herbie. 'Were you giving a lecture, too?'

'Me?' said Herbie. 'I was waiting for him to get the damn' thing over, so's we could go and have a drink.'

'Where were you waiting?'

'In the street outside. In the car.'

Devery reflected that there would be many cars in the quiet streets around the Lit and Phil rooms during a lecture. 'What time was the lecture over?'

'A quarter past nine he came out.'

'Why didn't you go for a drink instead of waiting?'

'I don't like to drink on my own.'

Devery returned his attention to Gabriel. 'What time did you start your lecture?'

'It should have been half past seven. It was a quarter to eight when we got going.'

'How did you come to be in touch with the Lit and Phil?'

'You'd better ask them about that. They got in touch with me.'

'Exactly *who* got in touch with you?'

'The secretary, Miss Buckle her name was. She had a gentleman with her, a Mr. Smallwood. They came to see me at the caravan. They'd heard about me.'

'Who from?'

'I don't know. I didn't ask.'

'When was this?'

'Soon after I arrived at Dodge City.'

Again Devery turned to look at Martineau. The chief inspector came forward. He and Gabriel took the measure of each other. They were both about the same height, and they could have worn each other's clothes without looking ridiculous.

'I'm going to get the Lit and Phil people here to identify you,' the policeman said. 'That all right with you?

'Up to a point it is. What will you tell them?'

'That you answer the description of a man we want, and that you claim an alibi.'

'That's fair enough,' Gabriel agreed.

Martineau became busy. He conferred with the duty inspector, and with Devery, and with Rosamund. Devery and the girl went out of the charge-room together, on separate errands.

The inspector busied himself in the matter of assembling an identification parade. Policemen in plain clothes were suitable subjects. Ten of them were gathered in the parade-room, and standing among them Gabriel and Herbie, in size, age, and general appearance, could have been plain-clothes men too.

When Martineau learned that the witnesses had arrived, he lined up the policemen, and told the two suspects that they could stand anywhere they liked in the line. Herbie selected a spot in the middle. Gabriel smiled and took the first place at the end of the line.

Mr. James Smallwood, President of the Literary and Philosophical Society, was brought into the room. Martineau stood near the door with him. 'Walk along the line,' he said, 'and put your hand on every man you know.'

Smallwood walked to Gabriel and touched him without hesitation. He walked along the line and touched no other man. He returned to Martineau.

'Who is that man?' the chief inspector asked.

'Mr. Lovell. He gave us a lecture to-night. Very interesting.'

Smallwood was taken out. Martineau advised the suspects to change their positions in the line. Herbie moved one place. Gabriel walked to the other end of the line.

Miss Prudence Buckle, Honorary Secretary, was brought in. She was a gaunt woman in her forties, who looked as if she were ready to make an issue of the matter, whatever it was. Her lips were pursed and her nostrils dilated as if she could smell something disgraceful. Her face did not change as she listened to Martineau. She walked quickly along the line of men, hardly seeming to look at them, hardly able to wait until she could get to Gabriel and reach out and touch him. She smiled at him. He smiled in return, and murmured a greeting.

'You know that man, Miss Buckle?'

'Yes,' came the clear reply. 'He is Mr. Lovell, who lectured to us to-night. And if you don't believe me I will bring fifty people to corroborate me. You've got the wrong man, Inspector. You ought to be more careful.'

Martineau's expression did not change. He allowed Miss Buckle to depart. There was a relaxation of the inevitable tension of an identification parade. The line of men began to break up. There was some talk, and a snatch of subdued laughter.

'Just a moment!' Martineau called. 'Get back into line, you men. There's one more witness yet.'

The men re-formed, and the suspects took up different positions. Policewoman Valentine entered the room, with Miss Muriel Naylor. Miss Naylor looked pale and harassed. The shock of the evening was having its effect.

Martineau gave her instructions in a voice which could be heard by everyone in the room. She moved forward, and walked along the line, and put her hand lightly on the lapel of Gabriel's coat. The gypsy smiled at her.

'You know that man, Miss Naylor?' the chief inspector asked.

'Yes. He's the man who broke into my house tonight.'

'Is he the man who attacked you?'

'Yes.'

'Are you quite sure?'

'I was never more sure of anything in my life,' said Miss Naylor.

## FIVE

DEVERY and Rosamund stood on the steps of the 'A' Division station, which was in the same building as Headquarters.

'As usual in this shower,' said the sergeant, 'we finish our day's work the day after we started it.'

'Go on with you,' the girl chided. 'It's only one o'clock.'

'That's what I mean.'

'Well, it was—interesting.'

'And it leaves us in an interesting dilemma. Whom do we believe? Miss Naylor, or the eminently respectable Secretary and President of the notably respectable Lit and Phil?'

'I believe Miss Naylor,' said Rosamund without hesitation. 'A woman couldn't have that happen to her and make a mistake in identity.'

'You could be right. But we couldn't hold him. The other people give him a cast-iron alibi.'

'Cast iron is known to be brittle.'

'Aye. Martineau might be able to break it. You can be sure he'll get at the truth of the matter one way or another.

'Well, I'll be getting along home.'

'It's late. I'd better see you home. I'll get a taxi.'

'You won't get a taxi on my account. It's a fine night, and I prefer to walk. I've been riding all day.'

'At this time of a Saturday night there are all kinds of characters about.'

'Then I'll make one more. I'm a policewoman. I'm not afraid of the dark.'

She said: 'Good night,' and briskly walked away. Devery sighed and let her go. He had an appointment, for which he was rather late. He had a mile to walk, in the opposite direction to Rosamund's. He set off. He was sure that Ella Bowie would still be expecting him.

Ella lived in a neighbourhood which he had always regarded as a strange and interesting part of town. Some parts of it were definitely tatty, others were prim and proper in fading opulence. It was a district of theatrical lodgings, and of maiden ladies who had dwelt there since King Teddy's reign; of dubious migrants, and of staid old-timers who could remember open fields round about. Ella lived in the middle of a terrace of roomy Victorian houses which had been turned into flats. Her flat was up one flight of stairs and, as no notably wealthy person lived on the premises, the street door was never locked.

As Devery approached the house he saw that there was no light in Ella's window. So it seemed that she had tired of waiting for him, and had gone to bed. Well, that had happened before, and she had still been glad to see him. He opened the street door, closed it carefully behind him, and went quietly up the stairs. He opened Ella's door with his key, and stepped into the flat. When he had closed and latched the door, he switched on the light and called softly: 'Hello there!'

Nobody answered his call, and he observed with surprise that the living-room curtains were not drawn. Amorous anticipation, which Ella could always rouse, began to die within him. The bedroom door was open. He walked to it, looked in, and switched on the light. The bed was tidy and undisturbed. He inspected the little bathroom and the even smaller kitchen. The whole place was neat, clean and deserted.

Wondering, he drew the curtains. This was something which had never happened before. It was no new thing for Ella to go to a party on Saturday night, but she had always made sure that he had known about it in advance, and usually he had been invited. Perhaps, he thought, she had just gone home for supper with one of the other girls, and would be home at any moment. The thought that she might be with another man did not enter his head. He was as certain as a man could be that Ella was faithful to him.

'Well, I'll have the kettle on when she comes,' he decided. He filled the electric kettle and switched it on. The water boiled. He made coffee. He realized that he was hungry, and he searched for food. He fried eggs and bacon, and had a midnight breakfast. When he had eaten the meal he cleared the table and washed up. He lit a cigarette and drank the last of the coffee.

He began to think that Ella had gone to a party with the intention of staying only an hour or so. She was having a drink and forgetting the flight of time. It might be three or four in the morning when she got home.

He lit another cigarette and had a tot of whisky from Ella's sideboard. He waited. At half past two he said: 'Ah well,' and fished in his pocket for an old envelope. He wrote a brief note and propped it on the shelf above the fireplace, then he turned out the lights and departed.

His way home took him through the heart of the city, and past the Northland Hotel. Without conscious intention he followed the route which Ella always took on her way to and from work. He did not expect to meet her.

As he turned into the last side street before Lacy Street he became aware of some commotion. This was Lyall Street, a thoroughfare of business premises and the small, rather shabby shops which catered for them. It was a narrow street with fairly high buildings, and as Devery entered this little canyon the first thing he saw was the blinding light of a photographer's flashbulb. The brief illumination threw into relief a line of vehicles at the kerb and a group of men near the entrance to an alley. All of them were tall or tallish men, and some of them wore uniform.

'A job,' the sergeant decided. Also, it occurred to him that someone might be curious about him; about what he was doing there at that time, and where he had been for the last two hours. Whether or not he was asked, and whether or not he told a good story, the tolerant and fairly accurate conclusion would be that he had been wenching. As an ambitious officer he did not want to get a reputation for wenching, even if it was deserved. He turned, with the intention of going another way.

The move betrayed him. He had been seen. Somebody called: 'You there! Just a minute!'

He turned again, and walked towards the group. As he drew near, a man said: 'It's Devery,' and when he arrived a sergeant in uniform asked half in jest:

'Where were you piking off to?'

'Home,' was the curt reply. 'I've had a hard day.'

'Well, nobody's stopping you,' the sergeant said.

'The damage is done. I'll see what this is while I'm here.'

Devery looked into the alley. It was a narrow, irregular passage flanked by small buildings which were mainly the premises of factors and wholesalers, a place of nooks and corners, open yards and little dead ends. Some way along the alley a gas lamp burned on a bracket. The mellow light revealed a figure which the sergeant knew very well. It was Martineau, still on duty.

'What's up?' he asked.

'Murder,' he was told. 'A woman got herself a neck shave.'

Icy fingers of premonition chilled Devery. 'Who is she?' he asked.

'A barmaid at the Northland, I heard somebody say.'

The sergeant in uniform spoke in sudden realization. 'You'll know her, Dev! Mrs. Bowie, Caps Bowie's widow. You remember that job, don't you?'

Devery was silent, stiff with shock. In the lamplit darkness his expression was not noticed. The bystanders merely saw a C.I.D. sergeant who was already considering aspects of a crime.

The uniformed sergeant went on: 'Nicest case of justifiable homicide you ever saw, when she did Caps. Self-defence so clear that them who had suspicions daren't make a murmur.' He turned to Devery. ' '*Course*, you remember! You were in the thick of the Plumber job with Martineau, weren't you?'

Devery could not trust his voice to speak without breaking. Without a by-your-leave he shouldered his way through the group and entered the alley. Again his conduct seemed to be entirely in character. Participation in the investigation of the Caps Bowie killing would naturally mean that he had a great interest in the murder of Caps' widow.

Martineau was looking down at something which could not be seen from the street. He turned at Devery's approach, and said: 'Oh, it's you.' He moved to meet him, and put out a hand to detain him.

'Yes, it's Ella,' he said, quietly and grimly. 'You don't need to see her.'

'I want to see her,' replied Devery, equally quiet, but determined. 'I can take it.'

'All right, but not before I've talked to you. I sent Cassidy to get you out of bed. You weren't at home. You signed off duty at one o'clock, and now it's going up to three.'

Devery said: 'You know how it is—it was—with Ella and me.'

'Yes, I know. And there may be others who know. Give an account of yourself.'

'I've been at Ella's place, waiting for her.'

'I want to know *all* your movements.'

'I understand, sir. I was in the company of Policewoman Valentine from two o'clock yesterday afternoon until one o'clock this morning, except when I went to get those two Lit and Phil witnesses. For that effort I had to take a Traffic car with a driver, P.C. Moorhouse. I was never out of his sight during that trip. After I left Policewoman Valentine at one o'clock I walked to Ella's flat, and waited there for a while. I have a key. I left a note on the mantelpiece before I came away.'

'What did you think had happened to her?'

'I thought she might have gone to a friend's house for

supper, and forgot the time. One of the other girls' houses, maybe.'

'Very good. You seem to be in the clear, because Ella was certainly killed before one o'clock.'

Devery was not quite himself. 'Suppose I hadn't been in the clear?' he asked bitterly.

Martineau perceived the trouble. He sympathized, but he did not feel inclined to put up with sentimental nonsense; not even from Devery, whom he trusted more than any other policeman.

'We would have had to examine your relations with her,' he said crisply. 'That would have stirred up something for the newspapers to make a fuss about. As it is, there may not be any need to mention you at all.'

Devery realized that he had been near to making a fool of himself. 'I think you're the only policeman who knows about myself and Ella,' he said. 'Cassidy may have made a good guess, and no doubt there will be some more good guessers.'

'What about Frank Horton at the Northland? And the rest of the staff?'

'They know I was friendly with her. Nothing more definite than that. She was just as careful as I was to keep things quiet. She knew we couldn't have gone on like that if people had started getting to know.'

'I'll talk to Frank, and show him you're in the clear. He'll talk to the girls. Happen they'll see that there's no point in dragging your name into it. The newspapers would make such a song and dance about it, it would be bad for the force. It's the force I'm thinking about, not you.'

'That's kind of you, sir,' said Devery, who did not believe that Martineau was worried about the reputation of the force.

'You'll have to try and act like any other copper. As if you scarcely knew the girl. When did you last see her?'

'Thursday night. But I spoke to her on the phone at teatime yesterday. Saturday, that is. She was expecting me tonight, however late it was. She said she had some information for me.'

'What sort of information?'

'She wouldn't tell me on the phone.'

'Mmmm. What did she think about your new partner? Was she jealous?'

'I don't think she knew. She never mentioned it and I didn't either. I was trying to keep it from her as long as I could.'

'Well, she'll never know now, poor girl.'

'Is it—rough?'

'I'm afraid it is. A razor job. I still say there's no need for you to see.'

'You told me I'd have to try and behave like any other copper '

'Very well.' Martineau turned and led the way to a recess in the alley. 'I'm waiting for the van, and then we can wrap up here till morning. Sergeant Bird and his gang have been and gone. The doctor too. He says the job was done between eleven and twelve.'

'One of Bird's boys was just taking his last picture as I arrived,' said Devery, trying to be natural, and then he was silent, aghast, as he looked into the recess.

The body, the poor crumpled body, was lying in a shadowed doorway. From the doorstep to the alley itself, filling most of the recess, there was a black pool on the concrete.

'Plenty of blood,' said Martineau coolly. 'The murderer stepped in it several times. He more or less wallowed in it.'

Devery made some sort of noise. His companion chose to regard it as a question. 'No, we haven't a clue. She was hit on the head before she was killed. The probability is that he waited for her, and grabbed her as she passed the end of the alley. He walloped her, then dragged her here to finish the job. The doc hasn't made a complete examination yet, but he's tolerably certain that there was no sexual interference.'

'Oh, oh,' said Devery.

53

'Robbery? Her handbag is there, see? It was lying there wide open, and it appeared to have been searched. There is no money in it. If we can prove that the murderer took her money, it's a hanging job even if it was only one-and-ninepence.'

Devery turned away.

'I think you'd better go home,' said Martineau. 'And if you can't sleep, better spend your time considering motives.'

# SIX

SUNDAY is traditionally the C.I.D. man's day of rest. When there are no major crimes on the current files, on Sundays the detective officers of Britain's city, county and borough police forces are served by only a small percentage of total personnel. On Sundays, as a rule, wanted criminals can breathe more freely.

But on the Sunday which was the day after a murder, a rape, and an important robbery, Chief Inspector Martineau presided over a beehive. His own squad had not been told that they had to put in an appearance, they just came. Other detectives, who might have felt that they were not implicated in Martineau's affairs, were told that they would be needed. Sergeant Bird's semi-scientific group was there, ready to help out with ordinary inquiries if necessary. The fraud squad was there. Even the divisional Coroner's officers were there.

Devery and Rosamund were not required for patrol work on Sunday, but Devery arrived at the police station at nine in the morning. He had not slept. He was hot-eyed and dry-mouthed, but not weary. He sat on a stool at the long desk in the main C.I.D. office, and stared at his open notebook. The same unending thoughts held him, as they had held him all night: the body, the blood, the smile of Gabriel Lovell, the candid eyes of Miss Naylor, Ella's empty flat, the certitude of Miss Prudence Buckle, the alley off Lyall Street, the blood. He was on a roundabout without motion, its screeching calliope the dying agony of a woman. He could not shut out a mental picture of a razor edge effortlessly slicing open soft flesh. He tried to summon reason for his own comfort. Ella had been killed by the weapon she dreaded, but she had been spared the sight of it. She had been knocked on the head first. There had been no terror, and no screaming. The sharp edge of the razor . . .

Martineau arrived, and Devery was thankful for his sane company. He followed the chief inspector to his office door, and was told to enter. Hard grey eyes considered him. 'You need something to pull you out of it,' was the decision.

'Such as what?' Devery already felt better.

'Such as work. I'll find you something to do in a minute.'

'How did you end up last night?'

'Flat on the deck. But I tied up every loose thread I could think of. I had a good night's sleep—three hours—without feeling that I had to sit up and make a note of something.'

'Tell me about the loose threads, sir.'

'Well, the rape job first, before the murder came up. I talked Herbie and the other fellow, Gabriel, into submitting to a search. They must have known they were clean, or they wouldn't have stood for it. I had their car searched while that was going on. Then, in view of Miss Naylor's attitude, I thought I'd better search that caravan of theirs. Gabriel wasn't having that. I told him he could agree to it or sit there till I got a search warrant, so he agreed. I sent Cassidy and Ducklin home with them to do the searching. They'll be here in a minute, I expect.'

'Is that all for the rape?'

'Yes, apart from statements. Today we'll take a closer look at that alibi. I couldn't do anything about it last night.'

'Then the—the other job came in, I suppose?'

'The murder job, you mean. Don't try to scrub round it every time, or else you'll develop a complex or something. Yes, the murder job came in. A P.C. on the beat found the body at twenty minutes past one. I did all I could on it. Last of all I went to Ella's place and looked around. I picked up your note and forgot to mention it to anybody, so you'd better forget about it, too.'

'Thank you, sir.'

'Don't thank me. It doesn't affect the job one way or the other. There's no point in making complications.'

There was a knock on the door, and Cassidy appeared, with Ducklin behind him.

'Ah,' said Martineau. 'Did you find anything?'

'At the caravan? No, sir, not a thing.'

'Did they say anything worth remembering?'

'If they did, they said it to each other on the way there. We followed their car. They drove straight into Dodge City and all among the caravans and old railway carriages, and we drove right on their tail. We were out of our car nearly as soon as they were out of theirs. Then we waited till they found their key, and went in. We searched thoroughly and didn't find a thing.'

'Whereabouts is the caravan?'

'It's right at the far side of Dodge City from the road, up against some bushes. They just managed to get their caravan in, from the look of things. The place is full.'

'I thought Boyton Council was trying to get people out of there, instead of letting them in.'

'So did I, sir. But they got in all right.'

'Did you see anybody moving about there?'

'At that time in the morning? No, sir. All was quiet.'

'Is it a nice caravan?'

'Yes, I'd say it was. Clean and well furnished. Not luxurious, but comfortable.'

'You said you waited while they found their key. Where was it, under a stone?'

'No. It seems they keep it in a special little place under one of the steps, but when the gypsy felt for it, it wasn't there. He said Herbie must have it, and Herbie said he didn't have it. He went through his pockets to prove it. I told the gypsy to feel in his own pockets, and sure enough he had the key. He unlocked the door and we went in.'

'And that was all? Have you anything to add, Ducklin?'

'No, sir,' the man replied, obviously trying hard to think of something which would prove his powers of observation, 'I think we saw all there was to see.'

Martineau nodded in dismissal, and the two detective officers went out of the room.

'I don't suppose they missed anything,' said Devery. 'If there *was* anything, it wouldn't be in the caravan.'

'Perhaps not,' said Martineau absently. 'I wish I'd gone myself.'

'You said you had a job for me.'

'Yes. Give me a few minutes to get myself organized. I think I'll have the caravan watched, it may get us a bit further forward.'

'How about Gabriel and Herbie? Are they worth a tail job?'

'They definitely are, if I can spare the men. I've got this murder, you know.'

'They're clear of that, at any rate. They have the best possible alibi. They were in the hands of the police.'

'Yes, they're clear of that. Let's see, I've got an interview with Miss Buckle at eleven o'clock. I'm going to dig a bit there.'

'What about the President, Smallwood?'

'No, I don't think so. He only heard of Gabriel from her. There was a gap in their programme, he told me. Some speaker who had to cry off at short notice. She had heard that there was an interesting man, an educated gypsy, recently arrived in Dodge City. He agreed to go with her and see the man. They went, and fixed it up for him to fill the gap. Gabriel is a good speaker, apparently. Not highbrow like most of their lecturers, but interesting and entertaining.'

'You're going to try and find out how Miss Buckle came to know of him?'

'That's right. The whole thing will be quite innocent, no doubt, but in the circumstances I've got to go into it. On general principles I'm going to pretend that it's mere routine, so as not to arouse any suspicions.'

'Miss Buckle was very positive in her identification, wasn't she? Does she know that Miss Naylor was equally positive?'

'She does not. I didn't let her set eyes on Miss Naylor. And there were no reporters around to start grabbing interviews and balling the job up. We're lucky in that respect. Saturday night and Sunday morning clear of reporters. Tonight they'll be in our hair.'

'There'll be men to go out on general inquiries around Lyall Street. Do you want me on that?'

'No. I want you first of all to go to Dodge City and nose around among the neighbours, but not too obtrusively. Then this afternoon, if you're not busy, I want you to phone Miss Naylor and ask if you can see her. Find out if she's still as positive about Gabriel. Get her afterthoughts, and so forth.'

'Very good, sir,' said Devery. 'I'm away.'

He went out into the main office, and was surprised to find Rosamund waiting there.

'Oy,' he said. 'This is your day off.'

'It's yours, too,' she replied.

'Suppose I hadn't turned up?'

'I suspected that you had. I rang in, and they told me you were here because there was a murder job. So I came to help. That's what we do in the C.I.D., isn't it?'

'All right. We've got something to do. We'll go and get the car.'

They found the Jaguar cleaned and polished and ready for the road. Devery took the wheel, and drove in the direction of the caravan encampment which was such a headache to the councillors and officials of the County Borough of Boyton. The trouble had started two years before, when the town council had proposed to build municipal houses on a cindered recreation ground which ran alongside a road which was the boundary between Boyton and the City of Granchester. The proposal had been met by a storm of protests by private householders, from both city and town, in the vicinity. There had also been letters in the papers condemning the proposal because it would rob local youth of a playing area. Furthermore, with the city not anxious to help because of the attitude of a number of its ratepayers, a difficulty about drains appeared.

So the scheme was held up, and during the period of indecision half a dozen families of caravanners were forcibly moved from some valuable spare ground near the centre of the town, a site which was required for a commercial building. The evicted families had nowhere to go, but they had to move. They set off without a destination in mind, and the officials, guarded by police, who had accomplished the eviction were so glad to see them go that they did not follow any distance.

The aimless route of four of the families took them along the road which passed the disputed recreation ground, and they elected to outspan there until they had decided where they would go. They outspanned, and to their delight they found a fire hydrant in borough territory which was fed by a city water main. How this came about no council engineer was subsequently able to explain, but there it was. The evicted families stayed and stayed, and moreover they were joined by others. Most of the newcomers were people who were under threat of eviction from sites in the city, and the city officials were glad to see them move over the boundary into Boyton. The city's water department refused to cut off the water because they declined to recognize the existence of the hydrant, and the town's water department could not cut off the water because it came from a city main. In six months there were three hundred caravans and makeshift dwellings on the recreation ground, and mass eviction appeared to be an impossibility.

The name of the shanty town came automatically. The inhabitants of Boyton were well acquainted, through radio and television, with the life and times of Mr. Matt Dillon. One day somebody uttered the name 'Dodge City', and everybody within hearing knew that he was referring to the trailer village. It was Dodge City, and known by no other name.

'Ever been in Dodge City?' Devery asked, as he drove slowly along the road beside the clustered caravans and obsolete railway carriages.

'No, I never have,' Rosamund replied.

'I have, once or twice. It's well named. Plenty of dodgers in there.'

'Where do we make a start?'

'I'm blessed if I know. These people dislike officialdom in any form. We'll just have to hunt around until we find somebody who has something to tell and wants to tell it.'

The car was overtaking a bare-headed, red-headed youth on a bicycle. The cycle was in glittering new condition, a sports model worth twenty pounds or more. It was much too large a model for its rider, who was about five feet tall. He straddled the machine grotesquely, swinging from one hip to the other as he pedalled along. First the whole of his weight was on one side of the crossbar, and then on the other side, and the machine was jerked about to maintain equilibrium.

'Get that character,' said Devery. 'That isn't his own bike.'

'Are you going to turn him up?' Rosamund asked.

'Sure. We'll find out whether it's borrowed or stolen.'

The car overtook the cyclist. Rosamund extended a hand and waved a 'slow-down' signal to the driver. She called: 'Pull in, young fellow.'

The lad looked at her in surprise, then his glance slid past her to Devery. He had already developed the thief's instinct—or else he had been born with it—of knowing a detective when he saw one. He braked sharply, stopped, and overbalanced. The machine fell to the ground but the rider did not. He had one foot on the ground and then two, and after that both feet did not touch the ground at the same time for quite a long while. He left the cycle lying in the road and fled, hurdling a low fence and disappearing into Dodge City.

Not unaccustomed to situations of this sort, Devery was not slow to move. He had the door open when the car stopped, and he took his foot off the brake to put it on the ground. He was out of the car and in pursuit of the youth without waste of time.

But his hopes were based on persistence rather than speed. Given a start, an active seventeen-year-old is hard to catch, and this one had fled with the bobbing agility of a frightened rabbit. But he had run into Dodge City and probably he lived there. He had bolted to his hole, and possibly it could be located.

As he cleared the fence the sergeant saw his quarry scuttle out of sight behind an abode which had once rolled proudly along the main line of the London, Midland and Scottish Railway, and after he too had passed the converted carriage he saw the red-head vanishing round the corner of a home-made trailer caravan. He also had to look where he was going, because Dodge City on a fine Sunday morning was a scene of abundant life. The course was littered with obstacles: children, babies in prams, washtubs, a waddling woman carrying clothes to a line, the line itself and its clinging wet burden, a tethered goat, a rabbit hutch, a heap of coke, another clothes-line, a large puddle of water of unguessable depth, and finally a mongrel dog which ran barking at the sergeant's heels.

Naturally the two running men attracted attention. People stared and commented, and a number of children joined in the chase. Devery ran through Dodge City, and when he thought he must surely come out at the other side a large black pool of water stopped him. It was deep enough for rubbish to float on the surface. Apparently the fleeing youth had gone straight through it and got his feet wet. Devery was wearing a good suit and his favourite shoes. He declined the hazard and lost the bicycle thief, temporarily.

When he had run round the edge of the pool Devery came up against a low wire fence with which one ambitious squatter had marked the extent of his claim. A house-proud man this. He was sitting on the step of his caravan, and he scowled when the detective stepped over the fence.

'Hey, I put that fence up to keep folk out,' he shouted.

Devery ignored the protest. 'Have you seen a little fellow with red hair?' he asked.

'What is he, Irish terrier?' came the sarcastic question.

Devery went over the fence at the other side of the squatter's ground, and looking around he perceived that he was indeed at the further side of Dodge City. The dwellings here had been arranged in a circle around the big puddle, with their doors facing it, and one of them had acknowledged the permanency of the stretch of dirty water by erecting a board at his door, and painting on it: 'Lakeside Lodge'.

Beyond this place there was a narrow road which ran along beside the wall of a factory, but nature had not been entirely conquered. A considerable clump of elderberry bushes was growing in what had been the furthest corner of the recreation ground. Someone had had to back his trailer right up against the bushes to make himself a place. It was a green-and-white job; not exceptionally smart, but the smartest in sight. Beside it stood an old blue Triumph car. The bicycle thief had led Devery to the home of Gabriel Lovell.

Devery observed that, and then his gaze settled on the bushes. Were they a hiding place? He passed between the car and the caravan, and went in among the bushes. The ground was well trampled, and that was to be expected with so many children about, but nevertheless the bushes were flourishing, thrusting out sappy growth with all the exuberance of elderberries in spring. The red-haired boy was not among the bushes.

Devery emerged, and stood looking around. A woman watched him from the steps of a trailer on the other side of the pond. She was in her early thirties, blowsily attractive and interested in a young man looking for somebody.

'Can't you make 'em hear?' she called. 'They're usually up at this time.'

He guessed that she was referring to Gabriel and Herbie. Whether or not she was a person of integrity, he could well imagine that she would have a gleam in her eye when the gypsy was near. He walked round the pool to get within speaking distance.

'I'm looking for a boy,' he said. 'A little 'un about seventeen, with red hair.'

'Well, he doesn't live here,' she told him. 'Them two is both big 'uns, and neither of 'em's ginger.'

'Do you know such a person?'

'As the ginger lad? No, I can't say as I do.'

She seemed ready to talk about the other two. He inclined his head towards the green-and-white caravan and asked: 'Do they have many visitors?'

'None at all as far as I know,' was the prompt reply.

He reflected that she had not witnessed the visit of Mr. Smallwood and Miss Buckle, or else she was purposely not mentioning it.

'Do you know 'em?' she asked.

'Gabriel and Herbie? Yes.'

'The big 'un, is he married?'

'He says he isn't.'

'Hah, they all say that. They don't bring girls home, I'll say that for 'em. But they don't half like to mind their own business. Door shut and curtains drawn all the time.'

'Is that so? I see they just managed to get their caravan in. I thought the corporation was trying to stop new settlers.'

'Yes. They'd no sooner dropped their trailer bar than the corporation man was at 'em. But the big 'un seemed to manage to talk him round. He's glib, is that one.'

'What corporation man is this?'

'I don't know his name. He has a flat cap on like a park ranger. He tries to stop folk from dumping rubbish, and that. He's always knocking about. Are you a corporation man?'

'No. I'm an inquiry agent.'

'Ah.' The woman displayed a worldly grin. 'Do you have to chase folk who do moonlight flits before they've paid for their furniture? You'll find plenty to do in Dodge City.'

'Yes, I'm beginning to think so.'

'Is that why you're after these two?'

'No. I don't think they owe money to anybody. I'm

after the red-haired boy, on a little matter concerning a bicycle.'

'What's his name?'

'I have a name for him,' said Devery grimly, 'but it isn't his real name.'

'Eeh, some of 'em are little devils, aren't they?'

The sergeant perceived that the woman had nothing more to tell him. He moved away, making his inquiries as he walked back to the Jaguar. He learned nothing of importance.

When he reached the car he shook his head in answer to Rosamund's questioning look. 'No, he slipped me,' he said. 'But at least we've got the bike. Property recovered.'

Then the police utility van arrived, and Devery learned that while Rosamund had stayed behind to look after the stolen property she had saved time by calling for the van to come and take it away.

'Good girl,' he said. 'We'll go along and see if we can find out where it was pinched.'

# SEVEN

Miss Prudence Buckle was punctual for her appointment with Chief Inspector Martineau. And not only was she punctual, she was fully prepared.

'I've been telephoning around to a few of my friends,' she said, when the chief inspector had seated her in a chair in his office. 'I have here the names of twelve women who are prepared to come and identify Mr. Lovell, if you should have any doubt.'

'Why do you think I would have any doubt, Miss Buckle?'

'Well, you had Mr. Lovell under arrest. It's awful.'

'He was unfortunate enough to answer the description of a man who had committed a serious crime. I told you that, remember?'

'And is he free now?'

'Oh yes, we let him go almost immediately. By the way, how did you come to engage him?'

The apparently innocent question brought an almost imperceptible change in Miss Buckle's expression: a faint suffusion which was not pretty. She hesitated, and then she said: 'Someone told us about him.'

'Someone told whom?'

'Well, I actually was the one who was told.'

'Who told you?'

'A friend.'

'I'm curious to know who this friend was.'

'I don't think I ought to tell you.'

'Why?' The monosyllable was blunt. There was no longer a pretence of idle curiosity.

'Well, everybody doesn't want to be mixed up with the police. I don't like it myself.'

'Yes. But assuming that Mr. Lovell is an honest man, what harm can there be in telling me how you heard of him?'

'Assuming that Mr. Lovell is an honest man, what *good* can there be in telling you?'

'Because I'm a policeman, and I'm not assuming. You're the one who thinks Mr. Lovell is honest.'

'And don't you?'

'I'll go so far as to say I don't know. There is other evidence, you see, which I can't disclose to you. There is a conflict of evidence, which I want to clear up.'

'Does Mr. Lovell know about this conflicting evidence?'

'He certainly does.'

'Can't he clear it up for you?'

'He can't, or he won't. I don't know which. If he is an entirely innocent man, he must be as puzzled as I am.'

'Well, I can't help you.'

'Ah, but you're just the one who can. Tell me who told you about Gabriel Lovell.'

'I will not. I refuse to involve anyone else in this.'

Martineau shook his head sorrowfully. 'You disappoint me, Miss Buckle. I would have thought that you'd be heart and soul for the interests of law and order.'

'I would be, normally,' the woman said unguardedly. 'But——' She stopped.

'But not when your own interests are involved, eh?' said the policeman blandly. 'All right, I won't trouble you further. Good day to you.'

Miss Buckle made a rather flustered departure, dropping her handbag and leaving her list of witnesses on the desk. Martineau picked up both for her, and bowed her out with slightly overdone politeness. He did not like her.

When she had gone he put his head out of his doorway and looked for an available detective in the main office. 'Evans,' he said. 'Follow that woman and stay with her till I arrange a relief for you. Don't let her spot you. Ring in every hour on the three-quarter hour.'

    .        .        .        .        .

The business of the investigation was in full swing, and soon, Martineau hoped, large and small items of information would be coming in. Personnel of the Criminal Record Office were seeking the names of Gabriel Lovell and Herbert Small in their files. In view of the possibility that they might be false names, P.C. Armstrong had the immense task of trying to find the faces of the two men among many thousands of photographs. He had been told to go on and on, or rather further and further back in time, for twenty years if necessary. If either of the men was innocent of a police record, he would scrutinize a million full-face and profile pictures before he gave up his task. In his spare moments Martineau also looked at photographs. He had a small neurosis in this matter, having once been badly let down by an inattentive officer. If his duties had allowed him to do so, he would have spent as much time as Armstrong with the picture books.

Officers were already busy in the vicinity of Lyall Street, and along the route which Ella Bowie would normally have taken from the Northland Hotel to Lyall Street. The staff of the hotel was being questioned. The manager, Frank Horton, and the barmaid who had usually worked with Ella in her bar, were due to be interviewed by Martineau. He considered that a list of the names or descriptions of men who had been in Ella's bar on Saturday night was an essential requisite.

.        .        .        .        .

As lunchtime approached, Devery said to his partner. 'I'll run you home, and pick you up later. There's no reason why you should miss your Sunday dinner.'

Rosamund agreed with the suggestion, and the sergeant drove through the sunny, Sunday-morning quietness to Shirwell. On the way, the girl asked for further details of the murder. She showed some interest in the personality of Ella Bowie.

'Women who get murdered,' she said. 'There's often something irregular in their lives. Did you know her?'

68

'I knew her very well.'

'Was she—attractive?'

'Very attractive,' said Devery, with a certain emphasis which made his companion turn her head to look at him. He told her the story of Ella Bowie and Caps Bowie.

'That would be before my time in the police, but I remember it vaguely,' Rosamund said.

Devery reflected that he had found the girl to be discreet and sensible. She would be working with him for another week. She might hear rumours within the force. It would be better for her to have the truth from him, and then she would have a clearer understanding of his own attitude to the murder, and of the special knowledge which he might be able to use.

'I'll tell you something in strictest confidence,' he said. 'It's something you need not repeat to anybody, and I want you to give me your word on that.'

'If as you say I *need* not repeat it, I give you my word,' said Rosamund gravely.

'Ella and I were—lovers. That's the only word for it. I wasn't courting her with a view to marriage, or anything like that. I would never have married her.'

There was a brief silence. He wondered if he had shocked the girl. How much of a prude was she?

'Did she know that you wouldn't marry her?' Rosamund asked quietly.

'Yes, she knew. I was on the level with her.'

'What would have happened, eventually?'

'We'll never know now, will we?'

'No. That was a silly question. Do you feel bad about losing her?'

'I did. I've been trying to think myself out of that frame of mind. It's something past and done with, which I couldn't have prevented. I'm trying to detach myself, and regard it as an ordinary murder job.'

Policewoman Valentine thought that sounded rather cold-blooded. A person should show some sympathy. For whom?

69

'Has she any children?' she asked.

'No, thank the Lord. She has no relation nearer than an uncle. He knows nothing about me. In fact I've never met him. He'll attend to the estate, such as it is, and I'll stay out of it.'

'That seems sensible,' Rosamund had to admit.

'So now you know the shadow in my murky past,' said Devery with just a trace of bitterness.

'Why did you tell me?'

'We're working together. I thought I'd clear the air.'

She let the matter drop. 'Take the first turning on the right,' she said.

Rosamund's father was in his tiny front garden, enjoying the sunshine and watching his tulips thrusting up green spears through soft brown earth. He was a contentedly plump little man with a cheerful air, though he had the worrying job of a mill manager in the cotton-spinning trade. When the car stopped at his gate he came out to it. Rosamund introduced him to Devery, and said that she had come home for dinner.

'And have you brought the sergeant to his dinner an' all?' he asked.

Rosamund was confused. 'Certainly, if he'd like to stay.'

Devery also was caught off balance. He hesitated. 'Thanks,' he said. 'I'd planned to go home for dinner.'

'You're in lodgings, aren't you?' Mr. Valentine persisted. 'I know what lodging-house dinners are like. You can have your dinner here, now you *are* here. A nice bit of roast sirloin and Yorkshire pudding, eh?'

The sergeant was so obviously tempted that Rosamund laughed at him. He also laughed. 'Well, if I won't be a nuisance,' he said, 'I'll be delighted.'

'I'll go and tell Mother we've got company,' said Mr. Valentine happily.

.        .        .        .        .

'It's a bad do, Gladys,' said Martineau.

'It's awful, Mr. Martineau. I can't hardly believe it.'

Gladys Potter, a slim, smart, nearly pretty girl of twenty-five or so, was the barmaid who had most of the time worked alongside Ella Bowie at the Northland Hotel. Gladys had been a barmaid for the whole of her working life, and for the last three years of that time she had been at the Northland. She was tolerant and wise about the ways of men as barmaids are, and she was normally self-possessed in their company, but today she was not normal. She was in the grip of mixed feelings. Ella had been her friend, and her eyes swollen with weeping showed that grief was the dominant emotion. The set of her small chin showed that there was determination too, a strong desire to see justice done in the matter of her murdered friend. Her attitude promised that she would help the police if she could. But in spite of her grief, sense of grievance, and innate decency, there was an irrepressible excitement and sense of importance. There had been a murder and she was in the middle of it.

'Whoever could have done that to her?' she wanted to know.

'Naturally we're trying to find out. You weren't working yesterday, were you?'

'No. We almost never get a Saturday off, you know. But there was this engagement party of my sister's last night, and Mr. Horton said I could have the day. But I saw Ella just for a minute. She'd asked me to get her some fancy buttons from Maxim's, and I slipped into the bar with 'em about half past twelve. She was all right then, and the buttons were just what she wanted.'

'Did she say anything which could be important? Anything at all?'

'No. There's nothing sticks in my mind.'

'Did you see Mr. Horton?'

'Yes. He was in there helping Ella. But I don't think he saw me. He was having a word with two fellows at the far end of the bar.'

'Having a word? You mean trouble?'

'Oh no. Just talking.'

71

'I see. Did you notice any of the customers?'

'Well, I looked round, like. I spoke to one or two of the regulars.'

Martineau asked for names, and Gladys gave them willingly. 'I suppose you'll have to find out everything you can,' she said.

'Yes. Who were the men at the end of the bar, talking to Mr. Horton?'

'I don't know their names. You'll have to ask him. They're strangers who've been in a few times lately. I've seen them talking to Mr. Horton before.'

Martineau was aware of a premonition: a sense of fate, almost. Here we go again, he thought.

'What were these strangers like?' he asked.

'One of 'em talks like a Welshman. A bit of a cheeky type. But the other's cheekier, without saying anything at all! It's the way he looks at you. He's bigger than the other, and ever so handsome. Like a king-size Cary Grant. He's always quietly dressed, like, but there's something about him. Personality plus. Lovely dark eyes he has, and sometimes when he comes in his eyes shine as if he's been taking a drug or summat.'

The change in Martineau's attitude may have been visible. Gladys stopped, and put a hand to her mouth. 'May I be forgiven!' she declared. 'Saying the poor man takes drugs when I don't know a thing about him.'

Martineau came out of his stillness with a smile. 'You're among friends, Gladys. Say what you like, I won't let you down. I realize that the mention of drugs was only a phrase to describe the man's appearance.'

Gladys was relieved. 'A silly thing to say, wasn't it? There aren't so many people take drugs. Not in this town, at any rate. But he does look a proper devil sometimes. Real attractive, you know. Nearly any woman could fall for him, I think.'

'What age are these two men?'

'In their thirties, both of them.'

'The dangerous age.'

72

Gladys shuddered, not entirely without pleasure. 'You're telling me,' she said.

Martineau laughed. 'I wasn't speaking of *amour*, I was thinking that men in their thirties are experienced enough to know what is going on, wise enough to guard their tongues, young enough to take a chance, spry enough to be able to do their stuff, and old enough to know how.'

'I daresay you're right,' Gladys admitted somewhat absently. 'I'm not sure whether or not I'd like to meet the big chap in a dark passage at night.'

Amused, but still intent on getting information, Martineau encouraged the girl to talk. But she gave him nothing more except gossip and general descriptions of people whom she had seen in Ella's bar. He took notes, and then he let Gladys go with a final reassurance that she was not to worry about what she had told him. 'Keep quiet, and you'll be all right,' he told her. 'If you see those two again, don't show too much interest in them.'

That made her cover her mouth again, as a horrifying notion came to her. 'You think that's what Ella did? Take too much notice?'

Martineau shook his head. 'We don't know. Those two might be perfectly all right. Don't take any chances and don't talk about them, that's all.'

But when Gladys had gone he sat in deep thought. It seemed to him that the barmaid's intuitive surmise about the motive for Ella's murder might not be far from the truth. She had had some knowledge, or she had seen some incident, which had made her a danger to desperate men. That was the answer *if* Ella's murder was not simply a maniac's crime.

'Well, Gabriel and Herbie are clear of that,' he mused. 'They made sure they were in the clear. They went to some trouble to be in the clear.'

    .     .     .     .     .

Martineau had always regarded Frank Horton, manager of the Northland Hotel, as a nice fellow and an honest man. He seemed to have all the confidence of an honest man when he entered the chief inspector's office and took the seat across the desk from him. ' 'Morning, Harry,' he said. 'I guessed you'd be wanting to see me.'

' 'Morning, Frank,' said Martineau. 'How's trade?'

'Busy today. The word got round. A lot of Ella's old customers looked in to say how sorry they were.'

'Yes, she was well liked. How long did she work at the Northland?'

'Fifteen years; man and boy, as they say. She was there when I took the place. She got married from there.'

'She went there when she was seventeen, then?'

'That's about right, I think. She knew the job backwards.'

'She knew a lot of things?'

There was a silence. 'Yes, she knew what was going on,' Horton admitted. Then he said: 'She didn't always keep it to herself.'

'Are you thinking of Devery?'

'Yes. Not that I minded. She never told him any of my business. Not that there was anything to tell.'

'I'll put you right about Devery. He was in this building, busy with a couple of so-called drunks, when Ella was done in. He was in the company of one or more fellow officers all the time from two in the afternoon till one in the morning.'

'I'm glad to hear it,' said Horton with apparent sincerity. 'He's a nice lad, is Devery.'

'Since he couldn't have done the killing, I'm trying to keep him right out of it. For the sake of the force. You know what the newspapers are.'

'Yes. I won't say anything.'

'What about your staff?'

'They don't know anything definite. Ella was discreet enough about *that*. But anyway I'll tell them not to go blowing to any reporters.'

'Right, thanks. I suppose your girls will be upset. I know Gladys is.'

'You've talked to her? Naturally you would. Well, I don't think I know anything she doesn't know.'

Martineau brought out his cigarettes and offered them to Horton. When both men were smoking, the policeman said: 'You *may* know more than Gladys. Yesterday may have been the crucial day. Gladys was off duty. You were helping Ella, I understand.'

'That's right, I was.'

'How was she?'

'All right, as far as I know. Absolutely normal, in fact.'

'She was on the phone with Devery around tea-time. She had some information for him.'

'So?'

'Could anyone have been listening?'

'I shouldn't think so. I remember the call. I don't think we had *any* customers in at that time. Was the information important?'

Martineau merely shook his head, and the movement could have meant anything. He was not prepared to tell Horton that Ella had kept her information to herself. He was not ready to reveal how short of information he was.

'How much time did you spend in the bar with her?' he asked.

'Oh, maybe a couple of hours altogether.'

'At what times?'

'She had a bit of a rush at lunchtime, between half past twelve and one. I was with her about twenty minutes then. I was with her again from about six o'clock till seven, in the early evening, and then from nine-fifteen or so till half past ten, for the last hour. The last rush kept us pretty busy.'

'Did you notice anything odd during those times?'

'Not a thing.'

'Were any of the customers particular friends of hers? Or did any of them seem to be?'

'No. There was nothing like that, that I noticed.'

'You know most of the regulars, of course. Were any of last night's customers particular friends of *yours*?'

The question took Horton by surprise, and for some reason it brought colour to his face. There was a pause before he shook his head and said: 'No. No particular friends of mine.'

'Any *enemies* of yours?'

'No. I don't think I have any enemies.'

'Try and remember whom you saw at various times. One way and another I'll know the lot of them eventually.'

Horton began to give the names of customers. There was another pause when he came to the end of his list. Then Martineau asked casually: 'Were Gabriel and Herbie in there last night?'

The hotel manager played for time. 'Gabriel and Herbie?'

'Gabriel Lovell and Herbert Small.'

'Have they been doing something?'

'I didn't say they'd been doing anything. I asked if they were in the Northland Hotel last night.'

'I don't remember seeing them. They were in at lunch-time.'

'Mmmm. Do you know them to talk to?'

'Yes. As customers.'

'Only as customers?'

'What are you getting at?' Horton was suddenly alert, and worried.

'Is Gabriel a sniffer? Or a hemp smoker?'

Horton was instantly at ease. 'I never noticed any signs. If I did, I'd have him out of the place. I won't stand for anything like that.'

'Does he get drunk?'

'Not to my knowledge. I've never seen him under the weather.'

'What's wrong with him, then?'

'I don't know that there's anything wrong with him. What makes you think there is?'

'You got your hackles up when I suggested that Gabriel

and Herbie were friends of yours. Before that, when I first mentioned them, you asked me if they'd been doing something. That indicates you think they were likely to have been doing something. In other words, they could be crooks.'

'When I asked you if they'd been doing something, I wasn't thinking they were crooks. I was thinking of something—er—just slightly illegal. Unlicensed dealing, or something of the sort. Those two seem to make a living without doing any regular work. Fellows like that are sometimes up to tricks. Sharp practice, if you like.'

'Have they tried any tricks on you?'

'No.'

'Have you done any deals with them?'

Horton was silent.

Martineau smiled. 'The manager of a hotel is usually obliged to get all his spirits from the brewery which owns the place,' he said. 'When managers do a bit of buying on the side it isn't a police matter. That's a good thing, because half of them are playing that game. Have Gabriel and Herbie been flogging whisky?'

Still Horton was silent. Whisky or gin sold in the manner suggested by Martineau might be stolen property. Martineau might be trying to get evidence of such a transaction. Any hotel manager who had bought stolen whisky, not knowing it to be stolen, was not likely to be subjected to criminal proceedings. Instead, he would be made a witness for the prosecution of the thieves. He would have to give evidence. His employers would learn that he had been 'buying on the side', and he would lose his job.

'All right, forget it,' said Martineau. 'Stolen whisky isn't what is bothering me at the present time. I'm more interested in the drug traffic. You can answer me without fear of getting into trouble. Have you ever heard Gabriel or Herbie mention drugs?'

'No,' said Horton.

'Not at all?'

'Not at all. Not so much as a word.'

'Very well,' said Martineau. 'You can go home and tell your staff that they'll never get into trouble by being discreet.'

.     .     .     .     .

During the afternoon Devery and Rosamund went to see Miss Naylor.

'You go first and see how she is,' the sergeant said as he stopped the Jaguar by the front gate of the little suburban house. 'She'll talk more freely to you, perhaps. You can call me in if you think it's necessary.'

Rosamund rang the bell at the front door, and was examined through the window by Miss Naylor. Then the door was opened.

'Come in, dear,' said the lady of the house. 'How nice of you to come and see me. Or is it some more questions?'

'I don't think there'll be many questions,' said Rosamund with a smile. 'I came to see how you were.'

Miss Naylor led the way into the living-room. 'Sit down, dear. Is that your car outside, with Sergeant Devery?'

'Yes. He thought it would be better if I saw you alone.'

'Very tactful of him, but I wouldn't have minded him coming in. I'll put the kettle on and we'll have some tea. I won't be a jiffy.'

She hurried into the kitchen and returned, and brought out cigarettes. 'I was just thinking,' she said.

'Yes?'

'About men. How they upset you. They run the show. Your boss is a man, my boss is a man. I try to have a place of my own where I can do as I like, and a man comes barging in and—— Shocking creatures, they are. They influence you and change your life whether you like it or not. Shall I pop outside and ask the sergeant if he'd like a cup of tea?'

'I wouldn't bother. He's all right where he is. It's a relief for me to get away from the men, too.'

'Yes.' Miss Naylor was thoughtful. 'I've wondered about

78

you, working with those enormous men all the time. Those enormous *young* men. Oh dear, I must be getting old.'

'Of course you're not getting old. They *are* young men. The oldest policemen aren't much over forty, you know. Most of them retire on pension before they're fifty.'

'Really? Your job must be very interesting, driving round with a sergeant. Is he married?'

'Most of them are, but he isn't.'

'I was going to say. His wife might not like it. I'm sure we should ask him in for a cup of tea.'

Rosamund could not persistently refuse hospitality for someone else. 'Well, of course, if you think so,' she said.

Miss Naylor went out to speak to Devery. He smiled up at her when she appeared beside the car. There was a brief talk. She returned almost in triumph, with the sergeant at her heels.

She made the tea, and served it. 'And how is our case going?' she asked with the animated air of a hostess.

Devery stirred his tea. 'We're having a certain amount of difficulty,' he said.

'But you arrested the man. I thought that was very clever of you, so soon.'

'Are you still absolutely certain he's the man?'

'Of course. Shouldn't I be?'

'The more certain you are, the better we like it. Unfortunately he has an alibi.'

'How can that be? Do you think I could possibly be mistaken?'

'In the circumstances, I don't see how you could be. Did he look different in any way from the man who attacked you?'

'Well, quieter and more civilized, but of course he was in the hands of the police. I'm quite sure he's the man.'

'In what way was he quieter and more civilized? I know he wasn't brandishing a razor, but I'd like you to try and be quite explicit. Apart from the fact that he wasn't menacing anybody, how was he different?'

'Well, his expression was different.'

'In what way?'

Miss Naylor frowned, slightly irritated. 'Well, his eyes were different. He looked quiter and more sensible altogether. I'd already told you he was nice-looking, but when I saw him in the police station I was surprised how nice he did look.'

'What was different about his eyes?'

'Well, when he was in this house they were sort of . . . Oh, I don't know how to describe them.'

'Would you say his eyes were mad?'

'Mad?' The idea that she had been outraged by a madman seemed to offend Miss Naylor a little. 'No, I wouldn't say mad. Sort of mischievous. Like a boy in mischief.'

'Did you notice the pupils of his eyes? Were they dilated? Or contracted?'

'I don't know. He had very dark eyes.'

'Distended pupils make eyes look darker.'

'You're thinking about drugs again, aren't you? I'm afraid I can't help you there.'

'That's perfectly all right. I don't want you to say anything unless you're quite sure.'

'Where does a man like that live?' asked Miss Naylor curiously. 'Has he got a wife and children?'

'So far as we know he isn't married. Have you ever heard of Dodge City?'

'Dodge City at Boyton? Of course.'

'He lives with another man in a caravan which is at present in Dodge City. He's a gypsy, you know.'

'Really!' Miss Naylor was astonished, and possibly she was rather pleased. 'What do they call him?'

'Gabriel Lovell.'

'Gabriel! A gypsy! Well, I never!'

·     ·     ·     ·     ·

In the car Devery said: 'Miss Naylor seems to be getting a sort of delayed satisfaction out of this rape job, one way and another.'

Rosamund was indignant. 'How can you say such a thing! After what happened! Really, you men have no idea!'

# EIGHT

ON MONDAY MORNING Devery and Rosamund went to Dodge City and located the corporation official who acted as general overseer of the place. He was an employee of the Public Health department, a young man, but already disillusioned. His name was Morton Jackson.

'It's like trying to empty the North Sea with a teaspoon,' he complained. 'One man can't look after this place.'

'What are your responsibilities, actually?' Devery asked with a sympathetic face.

'Well, I try to make 'em observe the general rules of hygiene. We don't want an outbreak of typhoid, you know. I try to get 'em to keep the place reasonably tidy. The police come to me if they want information about somebody, like you're doing. I also have to keep newcomers off the place if I can.'

'How do you do that?'

'If I can spot 'em before they get on to the ground, that's the best. In any case, I go and tell 'em to clear off. If they won't take my word for it, I get the police on the job. They clear 'em off.'

'I'm interested in two men who arrived here a few weeks ago. Gabriel Lovell and Herbie Small. Now, I'm not picking a fault with you, but is there any special reason why you didn't send them away as soon as they arrived?'

Morton Jackson coloured faintly. 'You've caught me with a leg up,' he admitted. 'That's the only caravan which has been let on to this place in six months.' He looked at Rosamund, as if her presence increased his embarrassment. 'You see, they'd got their caravan backed in nice and snug before I saw him. They just filled up an empty corner and

82

they weren't in anybody's way. However, according to orders I told them they'd better get hooked up and beat it.'

'And did they refuse?'

'Not exactly. Gabriel started to talk me round, reasonable like.'

Devery smiled.

'Yes,' said Jackson. 'He can talk a man off his hoss, can't he? I told him he might be able to charm the birds off the trees, but he wouldn't get anywhere with me.'

'But he persisted?'

'Well, he charmed a bird just to show me. He started twittering at a little bluetit, and soon he had a pair of 'em flying round and round his head. They just daren't light on his shoulder, but they were tempted.'

'They didn't *quite* trust him, eh?'

'Happen so. It was a startling thing, all the same. I asked him where he learned to do that, and he said it came natural: he'd done it when he was a lad. He's a gypsy, you see.'

'So I understand.'

'He said he never stayed long in one place. He said he'd be away in a week or two. So what with one thing and another I let him stop where he was. He'll be away one of these days, I expect.'

'Has there ever been more than two of them living in the caravan?'

'Not as I know of. Just Gabriel and Herbie, and they behave very well.'

'Have they ever had guests?'

'I've never seen any guests.'

'How do they make a living?'

'Ah, now you're asking me. It's a mystery.'

'Have you ever discussed them with anyone?'

'That Mrs. Humphreys started asking me about 'em, but if I'd known anything I wouldn't a-told her. It doesn't do for me to gossip with these people.'

'But the bird-charming impressed you. Haven't you told your friends about it?'

Jackson's glance flickered, and Devery knew that he was going to be evasive. 'Happen I've mentioned it the odd time,' he said.

'Where was that?'

'I don't see that it matters. It can't have anything to do with police.'

The sergeant wondered what Jackson was afraid of. The members of the Boyton Council were neither tyrants nor puritans, though there might be some higher official who was narrow-minded. 'You needn't be afraid of telling me anything,' he said. 'I won't get you into trouble.'

'You're a bobby, all the same.'

'I'm not a Boyton bobby. Neither is this young woman. We have no jurisdiction over you.'

Jackson had another good look at Rosamund. Perhaps he decided that she was trustworthy. 'I mentioned it just once at a club where I go,' he said. 'Fellows didn't seem to think it was much of a tale, so I didn't tell it again.'

'You must have had a bad audience,' said Devery. 'Some fellows, you can't tell them anything. They're not interested if they aren't doing the talking.'

'You're right there. I must a-been talking to the wrong fellows.'

'Who were they?'

'I don't want to give you the name of fellow members. It's a very strict club.'

'I don't want to know the name of the club,' said Devery, who already knew it. In Boyton there was a so-called working men's club which was extremely well conducted and, after a fashion, exclusive. It was notorious as a gambling club. No police spy had ever succeeded in getting into the premises. Any member known to have disclosed the names of fellow members to the police would be instantly barred.

'There's nothing to it, anyway,' said Jackson.

Devery suddenly perceived that it was more than a matter of mentioning the names of men who had happened to hear a story at a bar. While not a fool, Jackson was a man whose nature was the opposite of secretive. Possibly he had talked himself into trouble many a time. Typically, he had blundered by speaking of one particular place, his club. Now he was wishing that he had held his peace. And for a definite reason.

The sergeant reflected that one found gamblers in all walks of life. Here was a gambler with a steady job, but not overpaid. Any windfall in the shape of money would be instantly multiplied in his mind by the odds against some racehorse that he fancied, or by the length of a possible run of luck with dice or cards. Money was not only money to him, it was opportunity.

It was customary for policemen occasionally to pay for information: a distasteful but necessary duty. This, Devery thought, was one of the occasions. Whatever sum he paid for the information, he would be reimbursed.

'I'd just like to talk to you in private,' he said, taking Jackson's arm and drawing him aside. When they were a little distance from Rosamund he said: 'I'll make a bet with you. I'll bet you a quid that neither Gabriel nor Herbie has been in your club as a guest.'

'Neither?'

'That's right.'

Jackson considered. 'Bet me three quid,' he said.

'I'll bet you three quid if I learn the name of the member who took Gabriel or Herbie, or both of them, into the club.'

'Oh no. No bet.'

'Remember one thing. *Nobody* will ever know that you've told me. Nobody. Not even my guv'nor. Not even the girl back there. Three quid.'

There was a long silence.

'Three quid here and now,' Devery said.

'Show me the money.'

With a movement which could not be seen by Rosamund, Devery took a few folded notes from his pocket and peeled off three pounds. He slipped them into Jackson's ready hand.

'I've seen both Gabe and Herbie in the club, but not

together,' said Jackson. 'Both times they were with a fellow called Lewis Badger.'

'Thanks. You haven't a thing to worry about. What does Badger do for a living?'

'He's some sort of a dealer, that's all I know.'

'Is he a gambler?'

'Yes. He'll gamble on two flies crawling up a window. He's a funny chap. He knows poetry. Quotes it sometimes.'

'Where does he live?'

'Somewhere in the city, I don't know where. He comes out to Boyton, to the club, for a flutter on the cards. I'll tell you something. He was there when I told that tale about Gabe and the bluetits, but he never let on he knew him.'

'Right. Keep all this to yourself, and you'll be all right. Cheerio.'

With Rosamund, Devery returned to the Jaguar. 'What happened?' she asked. 'What did you say to him?'

'That's a secret,' said Devery. 'We never disclose our business with informers, though in this case you'll be able to guess everything. Nevertheless, I won't have told you. You'll hear me pass on my information to Mister Martineau, and then you'll keep your guesses to yourself. Fair enough?'

'Yes. It's all very mysterious. How did you persuade him to talk? Is there some secret method?'

'Oh, sure. That again you'll hear about. But mum's the word.'

When they arrived at Headquarters they went in to see Martineau. They found him frowning over records.

'Something new?' he asked.

'Gabriel and Herbie have a friend. His name is Lewis Badger. He has taken them separately to his club, which is a gambling club. Information price three pounds. The informer shall be nameless.'

'That *might* be worth three pounds,' the chief inspector admitted. 'Does it matter if I don't know the name of the club?'

'You'll have to guess, sir, as I have done. A gambling club in Boyton. A very strict club, I'm told.'

'I think I know the one. So you've got a job. Find out things about Lewis Badger, as discreetly as possible.'

'Very good, sir. Have you anything new?'

'No. Allowing for the chance that Gabriel might have a double, I've put C.R.O. on twins and brothers. And on gypsies.'

'Twins and brothers might be hard to find in the records, unless they've both been pinched together at some time.'

'I'm well aware of that, but I can live in hopes, can't I? Meanwhile, I can try and break that alibi.'

'What about the murder?'

'Not a thing. Just deadly routine,' said Martineau.

Devery and Rosamund left him then, and went to consult the telephone directory. Lewis Badger's name did not appear. They looked at the Burgess Roll, and found that Mr. Badger was not a ratepayer. They looked at local records. Apparently the man they sought had never been in the hands of the police.

'I do hope I have not been kidded to the tune of three nicker,' said Devery, in a tone which promised trouble for somebody.

'Badger might live in lodgings, or in a furnished room,' Rosamund suggested.

'Let's hope so,' the sergeant said. 'We'll sally forth and put out the private word, as opposed to the public word.'

So Devery went around consulting his regular informers, men whom he could trust not to pass on news which would result in Badger learning that the police were asking about him. Somewhat to Rosamund's mystification he kept leaving the car and disappearing into alleyways, into shops, into public houses and snack bars. Eventually he emerged from one of these places and winked solemnly at the girl as he got into the car.

'Badger lives somewhere on Trelawney Street, right in town,' he said. 'I still haven't found out how he makes a living, but he lives moderately well. Goes to the County Sporting Club every day. It seems to be true that he's never had trouble with our department, but a few years

back he was a main witness in a Gaming Act case which
hit the local headlines. Some associate of his refusing to
pay the bookie a few thousand quid he owed. Seemingly
he didn't come out of that job with a halo, but he wasn't
cast out of his club.'

'Trelawney Street next stop?' Rosamund asked.

'No. According to my information he should now be at
his club. We'll stake out somewhere near there and see if
we can spot him. The description is the same as Jackson's;
about fifty years old, medium height, "in fair round belly
with good capon lined", but not grossly so; dark hair, rather
sallow with aquiline features, usually wears a dark suit
and a bowler hat. A real city gent.'

'That description would fit a thousand city gents.'

'True. Anyway, we'll go to the club for a while, then
we'll have some lunch. We'll have a look at Trelawney
Street this afternoon.'

They went to the County Sporting Club, which had a
membership mainly composed of betting men and book-
makers but men nevertheless of some substance normally,
and of no ill repute. The club happened to be in Lyall
Street, not far from the scene of Ella Bowie's murder, and
there was still some police activity in the street. With
several obvious police cars at the kerb, the Jaguar could
stand unnoticed by people with guilty consciences. Devery
and Rosamund watched the club for a while, and saw
nobody whom they took to be Lewis Badger. They went
for their mid-day meal, and returned. It was nearly three
o'clock when Devery decided that they would go to
Trelawney Street.

The street was of a type which is found in every city and
large town. It was two rows of solid, well-built dwellings
gone from prosperous respectability to a sort of vagabond
commercialism. There were plates beside doors, but
they were not of the polished brass of professional men.
No less than three of the plates displayed the names of
quack doctors of different sorts, and there were two cor-
setieres. A turf accountant, a private investigator, a

spiritualist medium, a phrenologist and astrologist, a chimney sweep, a chiropodist, a veterinary surgeon, a teacher of pianoforte and a dancing teacher were mixed worthily and unworthily together. The houses which did not display name-plates were boarding houses, or flats, or rooming houses. The common characteristics of the street were a dinginess of curtains and a general neglect of paintwork. It was obviously a street where people did not know their neighbours.

Rosamund and Devery motored along the street without perceiving any obvious point at which it would be safe to start asking questions. Rosamund turned the car round and drove along the street again, and Devery saw Detective Constable Hearn looking at him with anxiety and undisguised reproach.

'Stop the car when you get round the corner,' Devery said.

When the girl had obeyed the instruction he told her: 'Walk back along there and you'll find a detective officer trying to hide himself in the doorway of D. Vavasour Smith, Patent Agent. Greet him with a smile as if he's only been waiting an hour for you, and then find out what he's doing there. This is too much of a coincidence.'

Rosamund went light-footed away, a trim, swift little figure which Devery turned in his seat to admire. He lit a cigarette and smoked it. She returned.

'He's trailing Prudence Buckle,' she reported. 'She's visiting at Number Seventeen. She was visiting there from seven till nine last night as well.'

'So, if Badger lives at Number Seventeen, it looks as if we know who recommended Gabriel to the Lit and Phil,' said Devery. 'And what good is that going to do us, I wonder?'

'Miss Buckle and Mr. Badger don't seem to go very well together, to my mind,' Rosamund commented.

'Strange bedfellows,' Devery agreed, and then he grinned when he saw the girl wondering how to take the remark. He added: 'We mustn't forget that Badger knows poetry. Maybe he and the Buckle spend their time quoting at each other.'

Rosamund was smiling. 'I wonder if Mr. Smallwood would indulge in gossip without passing it on to the lady?'

'That would be a risk,' the sergeant said. 'We'll have to get Martineau's permission before we approach him. In the meantime, we'll have to keep observations on Number Seventeen until La Buckle departs, then you can trip along there and ask if there's a Mr. Batty in residence. When they say: "No, but there's a Mr. Badger," you say you want Batty. Then you can try a few more houses just for cover, and come away.'

# NINE

JAMES SMALLWOOD lived in suburban Parkhulme, in a detached house which was bright with new paint. It was palpably the home of a man who lived a prosperous and well-ordered life. Devery went up to the door alone. That rarity of modern times, a maid in frilly cap and apron, answered the bell.

Mr. Smallwood was at home. Devery, a common police officer, was allowed to await him in the hall, where there was a hard period chair upon which he could rest if he liked. He remained standing.

All that was changed when Smallwood appeared. 'Come in here, Sergeant,' he said with a smile, and held open the door of a cosy study. 'Would you care for a drink? I do just keep a drop in here for my friends.'

Devery declined the drink and accepted a cigarette. When both men were seated before a cheerful little fire, Smallwood said: 'Are you still worried about that alibi? It's perfectly genuine, you know. I wouldn't lend myself to any sort of tomfoolery.'

'Nobody doubts your word, Mr. Smallwood,' Devery reassured him. 'I've come to see you about a different matter altogether. A confidential matter.'

'I'm an accountant. I can keep my mouth shut.'

'Have you ever heard of a man called Lewis Badger?'

'I have indeed. I used to know Lewis very well.'

'Used to? Was he at one time a member of the Lit and Phil?'

'Are we going to have the society dragged into something?'

'No, sir. Not in any way.'

'Ah. Well, Lewis was once a member. And I must say I liked him very much. He'd had an interesting life. Been a sailor. Seven times round the world, I believe. Then he lived for years in South America, and spoke Spanish quite well. Been in the United States for a year or two as well. Very interesting. It was while he was at sea that he became interested in poetry and good literature. He had nothing else to do in his spare time, I expect. Yes, I rather liked Lewis.'

'But he ceased to be a member?'

'Well, he got some very unsavoury publicity. He was revealed as a sort of—— Well, he was unsuitable. He must have realized that. He resigned without being asked. I haven't seen him since.'

'Did he have any particular friends in the society?'

'Well, as a matter of fact . . .' Smallwood allowed his voice to trail into silence. He peered at Devery. 'In view of Saturday night's affair,' he said, 'I can't help but put two and two together. Has this inquiry anything to do with Miss Buckle?'

'Only indirectly. Was she friendly with Badger?'

Smallwood chuckled. 'Some of the ladies seemed to think so. They smelled a romance. Then Lewis fell into disgrace and Miss Buckle dropped him like a hot potato. She never mentioned his name again, and everybody was careful not to speak of him in her presence. It was a disappointment for the poor—er—girl, I'm afraid. But it was better than finding out too late that she was linked to a man who was more or less a professional gambler. Some women wouldn't have minded, but Prudence Buckle wasn't one of them. She could have had no happiness with such a man.'

'Did she tell you how she discovered that Gabriel Lovell was a lecturing possibility?'

'Not explicitly. Someone had told her about him, she said. She sent a postcard, and he replied that he was interested. We offered him a fee, of course. Then Prudence asked me to go with her and see him, which I did. That's

92

all there is to it. I thought you hadn't come to see me about Lovell.'

'Nor have I, sir. That was just a point about which I was curious. The important item was Badger. I don't think it would be a good thing for Miss Buckle to know that the police were inquiring about him.'

'I'm sure it wouldn't,' said Smallwood, very drily for such a good-natured man. 'I don't need telling twice that a matter is confidential.'

'I'm sorry,' Devery said. 'We deal with all sorts, you know. We sometimes don't just realize when we're dealing with a gentleman.'

Smallwood was mollified, and they parted on good terms. Devery returned to the car, where Rosamund was waiting. As she drove the car back to town he told her what he had learned.

'So we seem to have discovered a clandestine love affair,' she commented.

Since Lewis Badger was one of four male roomers at No. 17 Trelawney Street, and Prudence Buckle having visited the house twice in two days for two or three hours each day, that seemed to be a reasonable assumption. When Badger had resigned from the Lit and Phil, Miss Buckle had *not* dropped him like a hot potato. She had merely ceased to mention him to her friends, and they had been afraid to mention him to her. So evasion had been unnecessary, though discretion had been practised. The handling of the affair indicated a certain amount of character, good or bad, in the secretary of the Lit and Phil.

'She pulled the wool over their eyes very neatly,' said Devery. 'Can you imagine how the old hens would cluck if they knew?'

The discovery of the Buckle–Badger liaison cleared the way to some interesting conjecture. Devery arranged it in his mind by putting it into words, not for Rosamund's benefit but for his own.

'Badger appears to be a man with two sides to his character. He's a gambler with a taste for matters of the intellect. One is a vocation and the other is a hobby. It *was* a *social* hobby, and probably he enjoyed intellectual chatter. There are millions of men with two sharply divided main activities, you know. Unfortunately, Badger's two traits couldn't be reconciled socially. He lived a double life, and possibly he didn't realize it until he got his name in the paper. After that, he had to content himself with being a gambler and a crypto-intellectual.'

Devery paused, and thought about what he had been saying. 'Miss Buckle remains his only intellectual contact,' he added, and shuddered slightly.

'*You* are a man with two sharply divided main activities,' Rosamund observed.

'Oh, I wasn't aware of it. What are they?'

'Talking and detecting.'

'Oh, quite,' said the sergeant, unabashed. 'You listen to me, and you'll learn. Now for the second lesson, and the big question. Is there also another side to Badger's character? Is he also a crook? I don't mean a petty crook, I mean a real, deep-dyed villain. Let us consider. Badger knows Lovell. Does he know him simply as a friend, or as a criminal associate? Is he the man who can supply the whisky which Lovell and Herbie have been trying to flog around the pubs, or is he criminally involved in a much more important way? We can assume that he recommended Gabriel to Miss Buckle as a lecturer. In the first place he may have done that quite innocently, to help his lady friend out of a difficulty and to put a few guineas in Gabriel's pocket. He knew that the Lit and Phil members would be interested in a talk about gypsy life, and he knew that Gabriel was quite capable of giving such a talk. Later, I think, either he or Gabriel perceived that the Lit and Phil was a perfect, gilt-edged alibi.'

'We don't even know that Gabriel needed an alibi yet,' said Rosamund.

'Be your age, dearie. Gabriel needed more than one alibi. He arranged to have two. And the second one was covering something very serious.'

'Like murder?'

'That's what I think. Fellows don't get themselves pulled in for drunk-in-charge unless they need an absolutely certain clearance for something important. Murder is important.'

'So Gabriel proved that he didn't commit murder and he didn't commit rape.'

'He didn't commit either crime *as a principal*. I'll lay any money he's involved.'

'But somebody else actually committed both crimes.'

'So we're looking for a double. A brother or a cousin.'

'But there doesn't seem to be one. Gabriel and Herbie have been living in Dodge City for weeks, and nobody has seen anybody with them.'

'They're keeping him well concealed, and that's a fact. But they can't do a job like Miss Naylor's with mirrors. There must be another man.'

'Why wasn't a mask worn, as it was on the B.M. job?'

'Because a distraught woman might snatch at a mask. Also the crook's personal vanity might be a factor. With an alibi worked somehow, a mask wouldn't be important. But with no alibi, imagine what would have happened if Miss Naylor had seen her attacker's face. She wouldn't have lived to tell the tale. Poor Ella didn't live, did she? I suspect she knew the alibi secret, whatever it is.'

'It's still a guess that she knew anything.'

'Agreed. If we keep on guessing we'll have the answers, eventually. Who actually committed Miss Naylor's job, the B.M. job and the murder? When we get one we'll get the lot, in my opinion. Friend Gabriel has been a bit too clever. By making sure that he couldn't be convicted for murder he got himself involved in it. But for that phony drunk job, he might never have been suspected of anything.'

'I suppose he didn't expect the C.I.D. to be present, and he certainly wouldn't expect to be put up for identification. He had a certain amount of bad luck.'

'I'll tell you something,' said Devery. 'His bad luck hasn't started yet.'

.　　　.　　　.　　　.　　　.

At Headquarters, Devery found that Martineau's ideas were running in a similar channel to his own. The chief inspector thought that the three main crimes were connected, and that all three would eventually be cleared. Moreover, he was hopeful about the eventual recovery of some of the stolen drugs.

'The heroin might be out of the country now, even though Customs have been on the look-out for it,' he said. 'But the cocaine will still be somewhere around. That wasn't part of the original order. They didn't take it at the first attempt, though it was there to take. The cocaine will help us to get a conviction, I think.'

'What's the programme with regard to Badger and Miss Buckle?' Devery wanted to know.

'I think we can leave Miss Buckle out of things from now on. She served her purpose by leading us to Badger. From now on Badger will be under twenty-four-hour surveillance. We'll soon know whether he's a sheep or a goat. He may be as innocent as a new-born lamb, but I don't think so. Gabriel and Herbie came to this town with connections ready made,' and it's my opinion he's one of them. I hope they'll lead us to the real heads of the ring, but I doubt if ever they will. Those fellows are too fly.'

'I suppose Interpol have been informed?'

'Naturally. And if we find the heroin in this country we might have an argument with the Federal Narcotics Bureau. If the stuff is destined for the United States, that is. They'll want us to let it go, so that they can catch the receiver with his hands full of it at the other end. Our evidence. So as it can be their evidence. It could be done, but it's risky letting all that value of stuff go. One slip, and we've lost it.'

'So what will you propose, if we do find the stuff?'

'Well, there's nothing like being optimistic. I've already had B.M. make up some little packages exactly the same in appearance as the ones which were stolen. I suggested that they fill 'em up with powdered alum or something of the sort. That way, we'll be ready for all eventualities. We might be lucky enough to find the stolen stuff before we're ready to make an arrest. If we find it parcelled up ready to go abroad, we can substitute the fake packets and let it go, so as to keep the enemy in ignorance while we carry on with the job. Not a terribly bright dodge, but workable. It might also put the cat among the pigeons on the other side. The receivers might see it as a deliberate swindle. It might make the members of the organization start cutting each other's throats.'

Devery winced. Martineau realized that there had been a slip of the tongue, but he did not apologize. He went on: 'From an international point of view the Yanks would have a good case. If we sent harmless stuff done up as heroin, they'd have no evidence against the receivers. They'd only be able to watch it go in, and have the consignees spotted as smeck merchants. They'll probably have them spotted already, so there wouldn't be much future in it for them. But that is what the procedure might have to be. The heroin is legally the property of B.M., wherever it is. It's costly stuff. If we can find it I don't see how we can risk letting it go out of the country without owner's permission. And I doubt if the owners would give permission. There's always a chance they might never get it back, even if the receivers are caught with it. It only needs two different departments at the port of destination to get at loggerheads, and the whole lot could be confiscated.'

Devery grinned. 'Don't worry. It might never happen.'

'The confounded stuff might already be on the high seas,' said Martineau. 'But my best bet is to act as if it isn't. I'll keep on pursuing the old routine.'

.     .     .     .     .

97

Two days passed in pursuit of routine. Detectives continued to ask questions near the scene of the murder, and in other quarters where their inquiries led them. Lewis Badger was kept under observation, and Devery and Rosamund helped with this task. Gabriel Lovell and Herbie, and their caravan, were also the subjects of an unremitting watch. P.C. Armstrong, and Martineau when he had the time, continued to look at photographs. The Criminal Record Office researched on brothers, twins and gypsies, but Gabriel's past was still a mystery. But Herbie was no problem at all to the C.R.O. He was revealed to have been the plague of Colwyn Bay, with convictions for almost every offence which had to do with the illegal acquisition of property.

With his usual luck, Devery was present when the clue to Gabriel's identity was found. He came down to the office on Wednesday morning, when Armstrong and Martineau were perusing files. With his hands in his pockets he stood looking over Armstrong's shoulder.

'My word,' he said, 'you've gone back far enough. If he's there, you should find him soon.'

Martineau looked at him, and then there was silence in the room. Armstrong turned pages, and Devery watched idly. Then Armstrong turned a page and the picture was there. The P.C. stared speechless at it. It was Devery's finger which came to rest upon it.

'Well, blow me down!' he said. 'Would you credit it! Lucifer Lavengro!'

Martineau looked up and growled at him. 'Yes, it's a funny name. There are plenty of funny names in this one, too.'

'Lavengro?' Devery mused aloud. 'I learned that name at school. George Borrow, wasn't it? I'd never have thought it was a real name.' And as Armstrong started to say something he commented: 'Rape, too.'

Martineau was on his feet, on his way over. 'Do you mean to say you've found him?'

'It couldn't be any other. Here he is in the days of his

98

youth. . . . Aged twenty-four years. The devil was handsome when young. Not half!'

Martineau stared at the full-face and profile photographs. Armstrong looked at Devery with reproach. 'Sorry, kid,' the sergeant said. 'I ruined your big moment. You found him, not me. I only gave tongue. Yours is the credit.'

'Bristol,' said Martineau. 'Twelve years ago. That makes him thirty-six now. Dead right. I wonder if there's an old hand in the Bristol C.I.D. who'll remember the inside story.'

The three of them trooped into Martineau's office. He picked up the telephone and asked the switchboard to put him in contact with the Bristol City Police. He lit a cigarette while he waited. 'Let's all have some coffee, Armstrong,' he said expansively. 'You've done well. Don't think I don't appreciate it.'

The P.C. smiled and left the room. '*Had* he spotted it?' Martineau asked quietly.

'Yes, sir, he undoubtedly had. He was gaping at it dumbfounded.'

'I'm glad,' the chief inspector said. 'He's worked hard. It's a pity you had to stick your nose in at the wrong moment.'

Then his Bristol call came through. 'I want to speak to the officer in charge of the C.I.D.,' he said.

He waited briefly, until a deep West Country voice announced: 'Detective Sergeant Higgins.'

'Chief Inspector Martineau, C.I.D. Granchester City.'

'Glad to know you, sir. I'm only temporarily in charge here, but I'll do what I can.'

'I want some information, and it means going back a few years.'

'I've been fifteen years in plain clothes.'

'Ah, you're getting your time in very nicely. Do you happen to remember a man called Lucifer Lavengro?'

'I certainly do. We had him on rape and robbery. Oh, it must have been ten years ago.'

'Twelve.'

'Twelve, is it? I am getting my time in, aren't I? We got him right, with a flock of witnesses. He admitted half the uncleared stuff we had in the books. It didn't matter to him, you see. He was insane. A real rough handful he was, too. He could wrestle a bit. I know a few people who weren't sorry when he was put away.'

'Where?'

'Lambham Hall, I think. He's still there, as far as I know.'

'What form does his insanity take?'

'I couldn't give it to you in medical terms. No *mens rea*, or something of the sort. The old M'Naghten Rules, I expect. I don't go for it myself. He was supposed to be stone doolally, but he was crafty enough in some ways. He wasn't as crafty as his brother, though.'

'His brother?'

'Gabriel Lavengro. Twin brother. Luce would do anything Gabe told him, and think it was the king of the gypsies talking.'

'Tell me more about Gabriel.'

'A real wide boy with a real wide smile. He was a wrestler too, but only for money. He never got into trouble for fighting. To tell you the truth, he never tripped up at all, though we think he did most of the jobs Luce admitted. The two of them were so much alike you couldn't tell the difference. Eye-witnesses who'd seen Gabe used to look at Luce and say: "That is the man." So Luce copped it for the lot, and Gabe was laughing up his sleeve. I haven't heard of him for years, by the way. Maybe he's up your way. If you think you've got Luce there, it's probably Gabe.'

'It is Gabe. He's operating in our parish, alias Gabriel Lovell. We're having identification trouble, too.'

Excitement came into Sergeant Higgins's voice. 'You've got a murder job, haven't you? A woman done with a razor. Is Gabe mixed up with that?'

'I'd like to be able to say "Yes", but I can't. He *is* connected with a rape job, though. As I said, we're having trouble with identification.'

'That's normal with the Lavengro brothers, but I can't see how they've worked it with Luce under hatches.'

'Neither can I. Are there any more brothers?'

'Not that I know of.'

'Any cousins?'

'There may be, but they'll be called Smith. I happen to know a bit of the family history, if you can call it that. I did hear—I wouldn't go on oath about it—that the old man wasn't a proper gypsy. His name was Smith, and he took up with gypsies and liked the life. I don't know if his wife was a gypsy either, but maybe she was. Anyway, Smith *looked* like a gypsy, and of course there are hundreds of Gypsy Smiths. Maybe he got fed up with it. He changed his name by deed poll, and called himself Lavengro. He had two sons and one daughter, Magdalene. She'll be married now, I expect. So far as we know, there are only two men called Lavengro out of that particular tribe.'

'The old man is dead?'

'Yes. Years ago.'

'Gabriel says he has nothing but gypsy blood in his veins.'

'What Gabriel says,' Higgins scoffed. 'I know him, you know. Or at least I did know him. The smiling devil. Anything he says is not necessarily untrue, but it's just as likely to be.'

'I see. Thanks a lot, Sergeant. Send me all the stuff you've got on Luce and Gabe, will you?'

'Yes. I'll send you the lot.'

'I don't think there's anything else I can ask you at the moment. If anything comes up I'll get in touch with you again.'

'Any time, sir. Only too pleased,' said Sergeant Higgins.

Martineau ended the call and turned to Devery. 'If brother Lucifer is still in a padded cell, we're back where we started.'

'He might be out now,' the sergeant said. 'He must be out. The identifications prove it. After an experience like she had, Miss Naylor wouldn't pick the wrong man.'

'After an experience like she had, Miss Naylor did pick the wrong man,' Martineau replied. 'If Luce is at large, he's the one who broke into her house. Gabriel was giving a lecture, remember? That must have been Gabriel. Somehow I can't see the Lit and Phil sitting for an hour and a half listening to a reformed lunatic.'

# TEN

MARTINEAU asked the switchboard operator to put him in touch with Lambham Hall Criminal Mental Hospital, and while he waited he drank his coffee. Though Lambham Hall was in Derbyshire, and much nearer than Bristol, it took twice as long for the connection to be made. But eventually he was in conversation with a telephone operator, and later with a woman who said that she was the Senior Almoner. She had a businesslike voice, so he assumed that she was an efficient person.

'I'm inquiring about a person called Lucifer Lavengro,' he said. 'I understand that he was a patient at Lambham Hall at one time.'

'He still is,' the woman replied instantly.

'He's still there?'

'I can see him at this moment through my window,' she said, and he imagined that she was smiling. The smile was not for Martineau, but for Lucifer. 'He's on the lawn outside, operating a mower.'

'Is he a good patient?'

'A model patient. He doesn't give us the least bit of trouble.'

Martineau thought that he detected the indulgence which the Lavengro brothers seemed to receive from the hardest of women.

'Has he been let out lately?' he asked. 'On leave or on holiday or anything like that?'

The woman's voice changed. 'All matters concerning our patients are confidential,' she snapped.

The policeman reflected that it was no contradiction in terms to say that she was aggressively defensive now. She

103

was a woman of a certain type. Very good at her job, and perhaps a little too keen. He understood her defensiveness. There had been questions in Parliament, and a lot of irresponsible blather in certain newspapers, about security arrangements at places like Lambham Hall.

'Your affairs might be confidential,' he said, 'but this is police business, and I require certain information.'

'How do I know you're a policeman? You might be a reporter.'

'If you won't take my word for it I'll wait until you have checked the source of this call. And if that won't do I'll come to Lambham Hall myself and see the principal.'

He heard the woman sniff. 'What sort of police business?'

'Very serious police business. It involves rape among other things.'

'So you're finding out about every poor creature who's ever been in trouble for that sort of thing?'

Martineau lost his temper. 'Never mind what I'm doing! Answer my question! Has Lucifer Lavengro been allowed out lately?'

'No, he has not. Is that definite enough for you? He's safe from such as you, thank goodness.'

'Then why the hell couldn't you say so in the first place?' Martineau bellowed, and then he realized that there was nobody listening at the other end. He put down the receiver and raved for several minutes about women who ought to have been strangled at birth.

'There are some women,' he concluded as he simmered down, 'who are absolutely unfit to hold any official position. They can't stand power, but they love it. They want to make a song and dance about the simplest question, sniffing around all the time for an affront to their bloody authority. They *love* making difficulties. I pity the poor girls who have to work under the authority of that hellcat.'

And having got that out of his system Martineau began to make preparations to delve into the history of the Lavengro family. There might be another brother, there might be a cousin who looked like Gabriel. To begin with he drafted a coldly authoritative letter to the Chief Almoner at Lambham Hall, demanding all available information about Lucifer Lavengro. 'I'll have the lot from her,' he said when he had finished dictating the letter. 'And if I don't get it she'll be in serious trouble.'

There were several more letters, to the police of Bristol and the counties of Somerset and Gloucester, to registrars in the west of England and to Somerset House. He also wrote to the two great clearing houses of crime in England, at Scotland Yard and Wakefield, for full information about *anybody* with the name of Lavengro.

.        .        .        .        .

Two separate details of two men were keeping Gabriel Lovell and Herbert Small under surveillance, and on that Wednesday they occasionally found themselves getting in each other's way. The reason for this was that the two men spent the day together. And since they moved around rapidly in the Hillman car, organized delegation of duties between the two teams was not possible. So it happened that sometimes Detective Cassidy found that he was trailing Detective Ducklin instead of the suspect, and sometimes Detective Cook had to content himself with shadowing Detective Evans.

There was one great consolation. The fine, mild spring weather persisted, and the city was a place of dusty sunbeams. The populace was in good humour. The traffic did not growl, it purred.

And it was an interesting day if eventually perplexing. The followers of Gabriel were pleased with it. The followers of Herbie, though excited at certain moments, were inclined to think that it was a runaround.

They had already found the pursuit of Herbie to be moderately rewarding. He was, when alone, either restless or nervous. He wandered around in unlikely places, and those places were duly noted. It was thought that they might eventually be places of some importance: he was looking at them to see if all was well. For instance, he had been down to the docks twice, and each time he had taken a long look at one certain ship, a big freighter called the *County of Warwick.* It had been ascertained that the ship was due to sail at the week-end with a mixed cargo, for New York, Savannah, Maracaybo, Santos and Buenos Aires. Herbie's concern for the ship heartened Martineau. It fed his hope that the stolen heroin was still in the police district which he was apt to describe as his manor. There was even a chance that arrangements had been made for Herbie to sail with the ship, to keep an eye on the heroin. Herbie was a coastwise Welshman who had served in the Royal Navy. He would not be out of his element at sea. With a faked seaman's ticket and a sweetened bo'sun he would be able to pass as an ordinary seaman at least.

On that Wednesday, in the forenoon before the public houses opened, Gabriel and Herbie went shopping. In the matter of groceries and meat Herbie appeared to be both buying agent and treasurer. There was nothing noteworthy about the errands until the Hillman stopped at the kerb beside a chemist's shop in a side street. There was some delay, a discussion apparently, and then Herbie got out of the car and entered the shop. He emerged a few minutes later with a small parcel which nevertheless was too big to go into his pocket. He did not put the parcel in the back of the car with the other purchases, but kept it with him in the front. One of the observers thought he saw the movement of Herbie giving the parcel to Gabriel, but he was not subsequently prepared to go on oath about this. The car went on its way. Detective Constable Cassidy was, at the moment, spare man of the double surveillance detail. He entered the chemist's shop.

It was a small shop, but it appeared to be well stocked. Unlike the big multiple drug stores on the main streets, it had the old-fashioned spicy smell of the apothecary establishments of Cassidy's childhood. There were no customers in the shop. Cassidy looked at the young girl behind the counter and decided that he did not want to frighten her. He smiled.

'That man who was in here a minute ago,' he said. 'What did he buy?'

He saw immediately that he had frightened the girl. Her mouth fell open and her eyes widened. Typically, she did not try to handle the situation, but rushed away into the back room without a word. Cassidy waited until she returned with the chemist, a small, stout young man with smooth ginger hair and a clean white overall.

He frowned at Cassidy. 'What do you want?'

Cassidy murmured: 'Police,' and briefly showed his warrant card. 'The young lady knows what I want,' he said tersely.

The chemist knew as well, apparently. 'Is there going to be some sort of trouble?' he asked.

'I don't know,' said Cassidy. 'What did you sell him?'

'I'm not obliged to tell you, am I?'

Cassidy shrugged. His smile was subtly changed. It pitied the chemist. It expressed Cassidy's slight sorrow over the fate of the chemist if he did not tell.

The chemist thought briefly. His face cleared as he made up his mind. 'I can't see that I did anything wrong,' he said. 'I sold him a hypodermic.'

'A hypodermic syringe?'

'Yes. His brother is a diabetic. Has to take insulin, you know. He dropped his syringe and broke it this morning.'

'That was what he told you?'

'Yes.'

'Did you believe him?'

'Why not? Mind you, you would think he'd buy his hypodermic where he was accustomed to getting his insulin. But I supplied him. I don't know of any law against it.'

'How big was it?'

'The usual size for that purpose. Two c.c.'

'How big is that?'

'I'll see if I have another one,' said the chemist. He went

into the back place and could be heard rummaging about. The girl stayed where she was, quite still, with eyes downcast. Cassidy studied her because she was the most interesting thing to look at. She was thin and pretty. Not many brains and not much vitality, he thought. Not his fancy. He liked a woman to have a woman's shape.

The chemist returned holding a box. He put it on the counter and opened it, and showed Cassidy a syringe.

'H'm,' said the detective. 'Bigger than I thought.' He took his little steel tape from his pocket and solemnly measured the syringe. He made a note and returned the book to his pocket.

'Will there be any trouble?' the chemist asked again.

'I think so,' said Cassidy. 'But not for you, if you and the young lady keep quiet. Don't say a word of this to anyone. If that man calls again for anything, don't give him the slightest clue that the police have been here. It's for your own good I'm telling you. He's the associate of a very dangerous man.'

'We won't say a word, Officer,' the chemist answered firmly. He was relieved to be able to help the police by remaining silent. He had done nothing wrong, but he had a guilty feeling because he had doubted the man's story, and had sensed that the intention was to use the syringe for some purpose other than the injection of insulin.

Cassidy went out of there, and found that he had lost the trail. He picked it up again after his opposite number had made a telephone contact with Headquarters, and he went to the square in front of the public library. The Hillman car was at the kerb near an outfitter's shop. Herbie was inside the shop, looking at shirts. Gabriel was nowhere in sight.

Alert, and afraid that Gabriel might be observing him from some doorway, Cassidy strolled round the nearest corner. Feeling safer there he looked about and spotted a C.I.D. car away down Boseley Street. Then, presently, he saw his colleague Ducklin beckoning him from a corner at the other side of the square. Herbie still appeared to be looking at shirts, so Cassidy took a chance and walked across.

'What's Herbie doing in the shop?' Ducklin wanted to know.

'Buying a shirt. Where's Gabe?'

'When Herbie went into the outfitter's he got out of the car and went across to the public library. He's in there now, or should be.'

'H'm,' said Cassidy. He had picked up the habit from Martineau, whom he respected. 'I wonder what sort of information he's seeking in there.'

'You can't risk it,' said Ducklin positively. 'You might run smack into him in the entrance.'

'I could find a side door.'

'If he's in the reference room and keeping his eyes open he'll see you as soon as you show your face in the doorway.'

'Arrah, you could be right,' Cassidy agreed reluctantly.

'You know I'm right,' said Ducklin. The risks which Cassidy liked to take were of the sort which got on Ducklin's nerves. Ducklin seldom took a chance and Cassidy often did. Ducklin was more frequently in trouble than Cassidy.

The argument was decisively settled by the appearance of Gabriel on the steps of the library. His apparently careless glance swept the square, but the two policemen were not in his view. 'The smiling bastard,' said Ducklin tensely as he pressed back against the wall.

Then it was half past eleven, and the public houses were open. Gabriel and Herbie had an hour and a half of wassail, then they went home to Dodge City.

.        .        .        .        .

That afternoon, when the reliefs were due to go out, it was found that Detective Constable Hearn's partner had 'gone sick'. Hearn was part of the detail which was keeping Lewis Badger under observation, and the work was too important to be left to one man. Martineau said to Devery: 'You and your girl friend had better team up with Hearn.'

This was an easy but unexciting assignment for Devery. As an old man of thirty, by far the oldest of the team and the one most likely to be known as a policeman by Badger, it would be his duty to follow in the car and let the other two do the leg work. The last contact by the Early Turn detail reported that Badger was at home. So Devery's team took over observations at Trelawney Street, with the sergeant round the corner in the car, Rosamund acting as liaison at the corner, and Hearn watching Badger's place from a little snack-bar across the street.

Hearn was a large and amiable young man who had done well in the police boxing championships. Everybody knew that Martineau loved him like a son, but nobody was jealous on that account because Martineau was determined not to show favour. He habitually treated Hearn more harshly than he treated, say, Ducklin, whom he did not like. At the snack-bar Hearn was known as a teetotal insurance agent who did not like his work. The proprietor of the snack-bar did not care who he was, or whose time he wasted there, so long as he purchased enough tea, coffee, sandwiches and cigarettes to pay the rent on his table. At the corner Rosamund had a telephone box which she could pretend to use, and a pin-table arcade into which she could disappear occasionally.

At half past two Miss Buckle appeared, and from the cover of the penny arcade Rosamund watched her with compassion as she entered Badger's lodging. There had been a new item of information about Badger. He was married to a woman whom he had not seen for years. Poor Miss Buckle.

At five minutes to four Miss Buckle reappeared and departed, and at four o'clock Badger emerged. He walked to York Road and waited at a bus-stop. Hearn had time to look at his watch, finish his coffee and exchange a few words of farewell with the snack-bar proprietor. He walked along the street to the corner, saw Badger at the bus-stop and waited out of sight.

A bus arrived and Badger boarded it. Hearn got the

number of the bus. He turned, and with a simultaneous gesture of both hands he called up both Rosamund and Devery. When they were all in the Jaguar Devery followed the bus. He followed it to the Somerset Square terminus in the heart of the city and saw Badger alight there. Sitting in the car the three police officers watched him. He bought a paper from a newsboy and appeared to read some items in the stop-press column.

'Getting the winners,' Hearn commented.

Badger's face gave no indication of success or failure with the horses. He returned the paper to the vendor as good as new and received a nod in acknowledgement. He strolled away in the direction of Lacy Street.

'Get out, Valentine,' said Devery. 'You'd better be on foot in case we get stuck in traffic.'

Rosamund obeyed. Hurrying along the crowded shopping street, temporarily not at all concerned about being seen, she followed Badger to the corner of Lacy Street.

He waited at the pedestrian crossing beside Maxim's store, then he crossed with a crowd. He sauntered along the further side of Lacy Street, then he turned left and was in Lyall Street. He moved along that thoroughfare in the opposite direction to which Devery had walked on the night of Ella Bowie's murder.

Rosamund had been quite close to her man in Lacy Street, but in comparatively quiet Lyall Street she crossed to the other side and dropped back sixty yards. When Badger stopped to look in the window of a tobacconist's she turned blindly into the nearest doorway. It was the showroom of a garment wholesaler. By the time Badger took his comprehensive and apparently casual look behind, she was screened from him by two panes of glass and a lay figure in a smart summer outfit.

She saw Badger walk on a few yards, turn suddenly to look back once more then go on his way. Rosamund emerged from her doorway just as Devery, in the Jaguar with Hearn, managed to cut across the main street traffic and enter Lyall Street.

Through the windscreen Devery saw Badger's distant figure walk past the end of the alley where Ella had been murdered. As a city denizen Badger would know what had happened in the alley, but he did not even turn his head to look. To the sergeant that omission was unnatural and vaguely sinister.

Rosamund also noticed Badger's strange lack of curiosity. Following the man's 'casing' of the street, it made her feel sure that he was a suspect worth following. She was conscious of anticlimax when he walked up a few steps and vanished through the portals of the County Sporting Club.

Rosamund turned and saw the Jaguar. She walked back to it, and got into the front seat beside Devery. Lolling in the back seat Hearn grinned and said: 'Tired already, sister?'

'I've come to report,' the girl said crisply. 'Very definitely he looked back twice. He's suspicious, or careful.'

'Did he see you?'

'I'm sure he didn't.'

Devery sat in thought. He knew quite a lot about the County Sporting Club. He was quite certain that Badger would not arrange to meet his partners in crime there. Then he qualified that certainty. Badger might meet the boss crook in the club, but he certainly would not meet any of the lower orders of crookdom. The probability was that he was not meeting anybody at all. It looked as if there would be a period of waiting for the observers, while he took his ease with his fellow clubmen.

But if Badger had merely intended to take his ease at his club, why had he looked back to see if he had followers?

'There's something queer here,' said Devery. 'We'll drive to the corner. Then we'll see him if he comes out of the back door. It opens into a dead end.'

He drove to the corner and reached it in time to see Badger in the distance, walking away along the street which ran parallel to Lacy Street.

'That's him, isn't it?' he asked calmly. 'He went straight through the club and out of the back door. He nearly shook us with the oldest gag in the business.'

As they pursued, they saw Badger's face when he looked back as he turned a corner. In that brief glance he could not have taken particular notice of the Jaguar, which was one of a dozen cars in his view, and by no means the nearest. Devery drove past the turning and saw him nearing the end of a block. Taking the next turning, he stopped and as soon as he was round the corner he waited, and was relieved when he saw his man cross the end of the block.

'All right,' he said. 'Both of you get after him, hand in hand. I'll follow on.'

They were still in the heart of the city, but had left the shopping area with its fringe of assorted business premises. Badger seemed to be making for the commercial district beyond the cathedral. Soon they were among big factories and warehouses, with here and there small streets where small concerns prospered or struggled, stayed and flourished or faded and vanished. Some of them were old-established, little firms which had served their useful purpose, without growing or diminishing, for more than half a century.

Rosamund and Hearn walked literally hand in hand, watching the sedate figure of Badger, who now seemed to be certain that he wasn't followed. Hearn made comments about what his wife would say if she could see him, but Rosamund kept her mind on her work. It was her attentiveness which prevented the subject from seeing them when at last he turned. What she noticed was nothing more than a subtle change in his gait. It was a sort of preliminary relaxation which warned her that he was nearing the end of his journey.

Where Rosamund and Hearn were walking at that moment, the flagged pavement had been replaced by concrete, to facilitate entrance to a repair garage. In the wide doorway of this establishment a young man in overalls was standing, having a good look at Rosamund. In the small show window on his right there was a secondhand sports car, an M.G.

'That's a nice car,' the girl said. She grasped Hearn's hand more firmly and pulled hard towards the garage. She caught him in mid-stride, and he lurched in the direction she wanted to go. They passed the garage hand. Grinning, he turned and watched them. They were safely in the garage when Badger took his last look back. It was a thorough survey of the street, but not even the garage hand was in sight. He had turned to attend to the prospective customers.

'Isn't it a lovely colour!' Rosamund exclaimed. She seemed to be looking at the car, but she could see Badger obliquely through glass.

The M.G. was coral-red, and its body was in good condition. Hearn looked at it absently, as realization of the girl's motives came to him. Then he looked at the price card on the windscreen. 'A bit dear,' he said.

The price of the car was four hundred and twenty-five pounds, and the garage hand was prepared to prove that it was worth every penny of the money. He was a man who did not habitually say 'sir' to any other man, and in any case Hearn did not seem to be of the type to appreciate that sort of blandishment.

'It's a snip,' he said, man to man. 'You ought to see it motor.'

'It's beautiful,' Rosamund urged, looking up wistfully into Hearn's face.

'Women always go by the looks of a car,' Hearn complained.

The garage hand grinned his agreement, but said: 'It looks good and *is* good. Not a thing wrong with it. Eighteen thousand miles, and one owner.'

'It's more than I want to spend.'

'It doesn't want a penny spending on it. Look at them tyres.'

Hearn looked at the tyres. He also took the opportunity of looking at Badger. The dealer was in the act of climbing three steps to a small door.

The garage hand adopted the manner of a conspirator. He looked around furtively and murmured: 'I happen to know the boss 'ud let it go for four fifteen. He wants it out to make room for a new Wolseley.'

Hearn tried to look like a man who was tempted. Devery and the Jaguar were due to arrive at any moment. It was important that the car should roll by without stopping. The garage hand would take a good look at it, and being a car person he might even guess, by a sort of sixth sense about cars, that it was a police vehicle. Also, though Badger was out of sight he might be watching the street through a window. Hearn hemmed and hawed.

The Jaguar went by, along the street without stopping, and round the corner.

'No,' Hearn said, reluctant but firm. 'I can't afford it, so there it is. Come on, girl.'

'Cheerio,' said the garage hand. 'Drop in any time. We might have summat more in your line.'

Rosamund and Hearn walked hand-in-hand along the street. 'Don't look across the road at all,' said Hearn, gazing fondly down at the girl.'

'Do you think I'm daft?' she demanded with a glance of adoration.

Round the corner they found Devery waiting for them.

# ELEVEN

BADGER appeared half an hour later, and Devery took off after him with Rosamund. Hearn remained, and at ten minutes past five he saw two men emerge from the doorway on the steps. They were a man of fifty and a young man in his early twenties, and they looked like father and son. Both men had the spare, active figures of men with a working life of constant movement if not actual hard labour. The older man was talking pontifically as he slammed the door behind him and he looked up at a window and uttered a remark which made his son laugh briefly. The father resumed his discourse as the pair walked away.

Hearn waited. There were two name-plates at the side of the little doorway. Furthermore, though it was still broad daylight, there was a light burning behind a dusty window on the second floor.

At half past five precisely the light was extinguished. Hearn moved further away from the building, to a position from which he could retreat without being seen.

A man appeared. He was short and stout, and though he was still of middle age he seemed to be in appalling physical shape. He slammed the door, shook it feebly and negotiated the three steps one at a time. This was a business which required all his attention; he had no time to look around. He did this when he was at the foot of the steps with both feet on the ground. It was a candid glance, in the manner of a local character who does what he likes and does not care who knows it.

Having looked around, the middle-aged old man bumbled away with tiny steps. Hearn allowed him to get out of sight, and then waited a while before he went to

116

look at the name-plates. They were 'J. E. Jones and Son, Bookbinders', and 'Sylvytex, Fine Fabrics'.

Having made a note of the names Hearn went with long strides in search of the bumbler. He picked him up in time to see him enter the Vintners Arms and turn to go into the saloon bar. 'Well,' he thought, 'that's that.' He went to Trelawney Street, where he rejoined Devery.

.        .        .        .        .

When Devery had arranged reliefs for a meal he went into Headquarters to report to Martineau. The chief inspector listened until the end, and then he reached for the file of observations.

'Abel Street,' he said. 'That rings a bell.'

He rapidly flicked over the typewritten sheets with his thumb. 'Here it is,' he murmured. 'And a note to see previous day, same subject. Yes. Herbie has been around there twice, to make sure the place hadn't burned down, I suppose.'

'So it might be significant.'

'It might be. We'll get a warrant and have a look at the place.'

'When?'

'When everybody is in bed. Will you be staying?'

'If I may, sir.'

'You may. It might be a long job if there's a lot of stock. We'll want Sergeant Bird. He's the boy for doing up parcels.'

'Right. Anything new?'

'Herbie bought a hypodermic syringe this morning, but he may have got it on Gabe's behalf.'

'Somebody's a main-liner!'

'Could be. It seems to be a rather big hypodermic. I don't know what size these addicts use.'

'It depends on the strength of the solution, probably. You remember Gabriel's shiny eyes? There was something in it, after all.'

'That wasn't Gabriel, that was his double. Or maybe it wasn't. He's worked a very smart dodge, somehow.'

'You didn't find him carrying any dope, at any rate. We might find it when we pull him in this time.'

'We're not going to pull him in just because he might have the odd snootful in his pocket. We want to get him right.'

'What's he been doing this week?'

'Nothing until this morning. Oh, he went to the public library to look something up very likely. With one thing and another it seems to me he's figuring a move of some sort. We may not have much longer to wait.'

'The week-end.'

'Perhaps Friday or Saturday again. Perhaps sooner.'

'The sooner the better,' said Devery. 'Now I'll get back to the job, and I'll come back here when the Night men have taken over. About what time for the Sylvytex job?'

'Midnight should be late enough,' said Martineau. 'Be here at a quarter to twelve.'

.        .        .        .        .

Just before midnight a car with three men and a driver set out for Abel Street. The passengers were Martineau, who held a brief-case, Devery, who carried a ring of master keys as big as a horse collar, and Sergeant Bird, who carried a cheap fibre attaché-case which was his own property.

As Martineau had foreseen, Abel Street was deserted, and all the buildings in its vicinity were dark and silent. The three men alighted, and the car went away. The chief inspector looked up at the Sylvytex building. 'There doesn't seem to be anyone at home,' he said solemnly. 'It's a good thing we have a warrant.'

Devery was looking at the door. He shook it gently to feel how closely it was held to the jamb. 'An ordinary latch,' he commented. 'I think I could open it more quickly with my 'loid.'

118

'Just open it, without damage, that's all I ask,' said Martineau.

Devery carefully put the ring of keys down on the doorstep, and felt in his pocket for the little case in which he kept his warrant card. The card was protected by a piece of transparent celluloid. He worked the celluloid in between door and jamb above the lock, then brought it down on the tongue of the lock. When he felt the tongue move he turned the doorknob and pushed open the door.

Martineau went up the steps with his flashlight in his hand. Inside, its beam played to the left on wooden stairs, to the right on a closed door, and forward along a passage to the rear. A sign on the door repeated the name of J. E. Jones, Bookbinder.

'We'll try this first,' said Martineau.

'You'll stand exactly where you are,' a firm voice told him, and there was a second beam of light on the scene. The three detective officers turned and saw that they were being addressed by a policeman in uniform. The man on the beat had caught them in the act.

'What do we do?' the chief inspector asked the others in feigned dismay. 'Shall we all set about him?'

The P.C. recognized him and smiled. 'Sorry, sir,' he said. His smile vanished as he went on: 'What is it? A job on my beat?'

'A search. You can give us a hand. Come inside and latch the door. Sit down on the steps and cool your daisies. If anybody else comes, let him walk in, then grab him and don't let go.'

'I'll do that, sir,' the P.C. said gratefully. He entered and closed the door.

Devery opened the bookbinder's door with his 'loid, and walked into a room which smelled of leather, glue and machine oil. Five minutes was enough to convince the searchers that Mr. Jones did all his business locally. His was not likely to be the place from which stolen drugs would be shipped.

The three went up the stairs and found three doors on a little landing. One led to a mop closet and the other screened a toilet. Devery tried the third door with his piece of celluloid, and shook his head.

'This is deadlocked,' he said. 'A very up-to-date job. I hope I can find a key to fit.'

'You'd better,' said Martineau. 'We don't want to be rousing a locksmith at this time of night.'

It took Devery ten minutes, by patient elimination, to find a key which would open the door. He led the way into a big room which was sparsely furnished. There was a long, wide table, a baling machine, some shelves, one filing cabinet, a desk, a chair and a stool. On the shelves were about a dozen silk 'pieces', and on the table were a partly used bale of packing canvas and a roll of waterproof paper, and three wrapped bales which might each have contained two pieces. The necessary cord, packing needles and labelling and stencilling equipment littered the rooms three window-sills.

'Not much stock,' Martineau commented. 'Just enough for a front.'

The beam of his torch moved around the windows. They were fitted with dark blinds. 'We'll have these blinds down,' he said, and when that had been done he switched on the lights.

The wrapped bales were of the first interest. All of them were addressed to *Sastreria Enrique Morales* at an address in Buenos Aires.

'The Argentine, not the States,' Sergeant Bird commented.

'Yes,' Martineau replied. 'If this is it, the Federal Narcotics question won't arise. We have no understanding with the Argentine, so we keep the stuff in England. Can you undo these bales and wrap 'em up again just as nice? We need to keep the other side in ignorance for a little while longer.'

Bird peered closely at the stitching on the canvas of the packed bales. 'I think so,' he said. He stood erect again and looked around. 'I'll make sure we have all the necessary materials before I start.'

Martineau sniffed the atmosphere of the room, then he walked to the desk and noticed cigarette butts on an ashtray. Tobacco ash was scattered liberally on the floor. So it was safe for him to smoke. He lit a cigarette, and began to examine the drawers and pigeon-holes of the desk. There was correspondence, but none of it related to the export of fine fabrics.

Devery was trying to open the filing cabinet. He failed to do so. He put his arms round it and picked it up and shook it. 'Empty, I think,' he said.

'Yes, it's a business which exists as a cover,' Martineau said. 'He sends a few bales out when he has some smeck to go. You get the idea? There's a high duty on silk. These people think that Customs officers will be less suspicious of a bale on which a high duty is already payable.'

He had found some letterheads, and now, turning down in a bottom drawer, he found some older ones.

'It isn't a new business, at any rate,' he said. 'It's been in existence for a number of years. Probably it was legitimate at one time. This Thomas Tiffany named here has been the sole proprietor all along, by the look of things. Maybe he had a few bad years, then he found a new line; small consignments and large returns.'

'It doesn't look as if we'll get in touch with the heads of the job through this place. It's just a packing station.'

'Important, nevertheless. This man might be the pivot of the organization. He might even have a book of addresses somewhere.'

'I doubt it, sir.'

'You do right to doubt. We might be kidding ourselves. We haven't found *anything* yet.'

With that the chief inspector went over to Bird, who was busy at some scales which he had found in a corner of the room. 'These parcels are all the same weight,' said Bird. 'They don't intend to be caught that way.'

He began to open one of the bales. Martineau watched

him. Devery examined the unwrapped pieces on the shelves, taking care to leave each one exactly as he had found it.

The first bale contained two bolts of silk and nothing more. Working deftly but carefully Bird began to repack it.

'Aren't you going to open the others first?' Martineau demanded.

Bird shook his head. 'Not till I've done this one up. They're all exactly alike in appearance. I must have copies to work with. It'll be a long job, sir. I've got to duplicate the stitches in the canvas. The same holes, see? Luckily that isn't too difficult when you're stitching with cord.'

So Martineau had to wait. Bird opened and repacked the second bale which contained nothing but silk. Both Devery and the chief inspector watched anxiously as the third bale was opened. It had been skilfully faked to be the same size as the others, but it had a hollow in the middle, stiffened by corrugated cardboard. Bird unrolled the cardboard and found a parcel wrapped in cellophane. The parcel contained a number of small packages.

Martineau counted them. 'Forty-seven,' he said with forced calm. 'This is the whole of the B.M. heroin, still bearing the same labels.'

He put the packages carefully on one side and opened his brief-case, which was filled with packages of the same appearance as the ones taken from the bale.

'Replace with exactly forty-seven of these,' he said. 'When these get to Buenos Aires our old friend Sastreria will find he's been done, and done proper. I hope he distributes it and ruins his business before he finds out what it is.'

While Bird was repacking the third bale, Martineau was writing his initials on each one of the packages of heroin.

'I hope it *is* heroin, and not an ultra-clever gag by pal Gabriel,' he said. 'Come on, Devery, put your personal mark of identification on these packets. You too, Bird, when you're ready.'

When all was done, Bird carefully picked up every piece

of wasted string. He replaced the packing needle exactly where he had found it.

'He won't be able to tell?' Martineau queried.

Bird looked at the three bales. 'I've put them back exactly where they were to the inch,' he said. 'But he may be able to tell his own stitching from mine if he looks closely.'

'We'll have to chance that. It won't be the end of everything if he does find out, but it'll be a lot better if he doesn't. We need to keep him in a state of not knowing, until we've got the job properly set up.'

'It seems a pity,' said Devery.

'Ah, you want to start locking people up right and left. What's the hurry? We've got this fellow toasting nicely. We'll leave him to get brown all over. I want Gabriel first. He's my boy.'

He inclined his head to the telephone on the desk. 'Call us a car,' he said. 'Mr. Tiffany won't mind if we use his phone. Especially if he never knows about it.'

# TWELVE

On that same still April night two detective constables maintained a vigil on a trailer caravan in Dodge City. It was not a comfortable assignment, but both men admitted that it could have been worse. They were in a store shed in a factory yard, and they took turns in standing on a crate and looking through a high window. This gave them a view over the factory wall and across the road which was the back boundary of the squatters' village. A waning moon gave them some light, and they could see Gabriel Lovell's caravan and part of the little elderberry copse whose branches touched its rear end, and the Hillman car which stood near. Since midnight the watchers had opened a window so that they could feel to be in touch with the outdoors. The night silence crept into the room and soothed them. They talked only occasionally, in undertones.

Technically they were 'trespassing' in the police district of Boyton, but they were within five hundred yards of their own city boundary, and they still had power to act as policemen. The factory wall was a bar to a quick sortie on their part, and to counteract this handicap they were equipped with a field radio tuned in to Headquarters. They could pass on information which could be relayed to a car waiting on city territory near the main entrance to the settlement.

They had passed on no information. Since nightfall the caravan had been dark. Its windows were so efficiently curtained that it was impossible to tell from any distance whether or not the interior was lighted. During the early evening Gabriel and Herbie had gone into the city, where they had spent several hours in several public houses. They had returned to Dodge City after closing time, and for a minute or two they had shown a light by leaving open the door of the caravan. Then the door had been closed, and nothing more had been seen.

That was the situation at three in the morning, and naturally the watchers did not expect to see anything more until a long time after daybreak. Nevertheless, the vigil was being maintained according to orders. Standing on the crate was a detective called Wallace, a thickset man of forty who had allowed himself to put on weight to the extent that now he did not like to run. His companion, Fisher, sat on another crate and smoked a cigarette. He was young, still in his twenties, long-legged, lean and restless. This sort of waiting work was punishment for Fisher. It had been said of him that he would rather run than walk.

At three o'clock Wallace was facing the window and looking inward at his own thoughts. He heard no sound from the Lovell caravan, but his reverie was shattered when he saw a beam of light from its doorway. Before he mentioned the matter to his companion he made sure that it was not an illusion caused by an unexpected spell of sleepiness.

'Quiet,' he whispered. 'There's something stirring.'

Fisher was standing beside him in an instant. They saw two figures appear in the doorway of the caravan. At first there appeared to be a struggle, and then it could be seen that one was supporting the other. They unsteadily negotiated the steps from the door, and reeled towards the car. One of them could be heard mumbling. The other one said in an ordinary tone audible only because the night was so quiet: 'The nearest hospital for you, Herbie, my boy.'

'Shut that window,' Wallace hissed. 'We'll have to get cracking with the walkie-talkie.'

Fisher went to the window and closed it silently. 'I'll try and get to the car,' he said, and he vanished like a shadow through the doorway of the shed.

Wallace got the attention of Headquarters. 'Subjects

have left caravan and gone to their car,' he reported. 'One of them appears to be in a state of collapse. The other was heard to say: "Hospital for you, Herbie," so assume sick man is Small. Lovell is now putting Small in front seat of car. He has closed door of car and gone back to caravan and entered. Now he is emerging again, carrying some small object down by his side. I can't see what it is. He has closed door of caravan without turning off the light. He is getting into driver's seat of car. Now he is driving away towards main entrance. Please ask Constable Nash, Car Seventeen, to delay pursuit of subject car as long as possible because Constable Fisher is on the way to join him. End of message.'

Fisher had run silently to the end of the factory yard and climbed the gate, and he was about a third of the way across the settlement when he heard Gabriel start the Hillman. He was unable to increase his pace. He just ran on as fast as he could while the car overtook him and passed him on a parallel course. He heard it slow down at the main road and, a moment later, accelerate away. But then he had not far to go. Whether he caught the police car depended on how much start Nash was prepared to concede to Gabriel.

Fisher hurdled the fence into the main road and saw a car without lights rolling towards him. The driver saw him, and stopped. He tumbled into the front seat and the car shot away before he had closed the door.

'You just made it,' said Nash. 'I couldn't have given you another second. Though what it matters if he's only going to hospital I don't know.'

Fisher found enough breath to speak. 'What hospital? Is this the way he's going?'

'There's his tail light, look. He must be going to Boyton Infirmary.'

Fisher sank back in his seat and watched the light ahead. Nash did not have to drive very fast to keep it in sight. They turned into Boyton Old Road and headed for the centre of the town. They passed the Royal Infirmary without stopping.

126

'What now?' Nash wanted to know. 'Going this way it's a day's march to the next hospital.'

'Are you sure we're following the right car?'

'I've had him in sight every second except when he turned a couple of corners. There's no other traffic about. It's bound to be the right car.'

'It's the only one we've got, anyway,' Fisher rejoined in a tone of agreement. He used the radio to tell Headquarters what was happening.

The Hillman went right through Boyton and began to climb up towards the moors. 'This is a right how-de-do,' moaned Nash, worried about jurisdiction. 'We shall be in Yorkshire before we know where we are.'

'Let's obey orders, and somebody else can do the worrying,' said Fisher comfortably. He was moving across the earth's surface, and he was content. This was a lot better than sitting on a dusty crate in a dusty storeroom where nothing but the spiders moved.

On and on went the two cars until they were away on the open moors and very definitely in the next county. The voice of Headquarters faded, because the city police radio was not designed to operate over any distance. But before radio contact was finally broken, Nash was heartened by instructions to follow the Hillman to hell and back if necessary.

At the height of land, where the road ran like a grey ribbon across a dark slope, Nash saw Gabriel's tail light suddenly vanish. He braked and then drove forward cautiously.

'I see it,' said Fisher. 'Standing without lights.'

Nash immediately put the police car into reverse gear. He backed away some distance. 'If we can see him he can see us,' he remarked.

'I noticed a side road a bit further back,' said Fisher. 'It looked like one of those old quarry roads. Suppose we put the car up there out of sight. Then you can lie in the heather and watch the road, and I'll go scouting on foot.'

'I think I'd better go with you. It looks damned queer. What's he brought a sick man all the way up here for?'

'You think he's dead?'

'Sure. It's a burying job.'

'I think we're on to something big, anyway. All right, we'll leave the car.'

'We'll have to be careful. We're liable to be made fools of, playing hide-and-seek with a gypsy, in the country, in the dark.'

The two men went back and found the quarry road, and hid their car. Then they went towards the Hillman, and as soon as they could discern it they took to the heather, going cautiously over the rough ground and making sure that they did not at any time appear against the sky line.

They stopped at the crest of a low ridge, with the Hillman almost directly abeam of them. Nash got down on hands and knees, and tugged at Fisher's sleeve for him to do likewise. Fisher stretched at full length and crawled forward to look over the other side. He saw a declivity which was all humps and hollows: heather, bilberry, cotton grass, bracken and bent; bare peat hag; rocks; little gullies and little hillocks. He could discern no movement. The two men lay still, watching, both of them afraid that they had ruined the operation by letting themselves be seen or heard. Both of them were full of query and comment, but they dared not speak. And they dared not go further. With Herbie's heavy body to handle, Gabriel could not be far away.

It was pleasant lying in the heather. The moorland air was balm to the lungs of city men. It was cool, but by no means cold. Nash could have slept. Fisher had never been more wide awake.

They waited, and the pallid moonlight changed to the first greyness of the slow English daybreak. A skylark, the real harbinger of dawn, climbed trilling until he was out of sight. Minutes later, the first distant farmyard cock cleared his throat.

Fisher could contain himself no longer. 'What the hell's going on?' he wanted to know.

'Waiting for daylight, happen,' Nash breathed.

'In that case we'd better get out of it. We'll be stuck up here like bottles on a wall.'

Nash did not move. Fisher drew back from the crest of the ridge and sat up. He looked around carefully, then moved off towards higher ground, making for a place where the ridge joined a sloping plateau.

At this point he lay flat, dragging himself to a spot from which he could see. There was nothing but deserted waste-land. His view of it grew clearer as the darkness reluctantly receded, and he perceived that the ground started to fall away at a distance of about four hundred yards. He had a longing to see what was there, out of sight, but it was too far to walk in the open, and too far to crawl.

Then it was broad daylight, and the eastern skyline was very bright. Fisher perceived that soon he would be looking into the eye of the sun. If the man he sought appeared from that direction, he might fail to see him first. He moved to a clump of gorse, so that it would be between him and the sun.

Presently a great radiance on the skyline showed him where the sun would appear. Into that radiance walked Gabriel. As he climbed from whatever valley there was on the other side of the little plateau, first his head, then his shoulders appeared. Then he was up on the plateau, but still at a lower level than the man who watched him. He climbed like a weary man and drooped as he stood to look back. He looked down, a black figure contemplating a deed done.

Then he turned and gazed around, and Fisher flattened himself behind the gorse. He began to trudge along the edge of the plateau, still climbing. Fisher began to sweat. If Nash had not moved, he would soon be in Gabriel's view.

Halfway across the plateau Gabriel stopped, and took another long look around. He gave no sign of having seen Nash, and evidently he decided to climb no further. He turned away downhill, going straight towards the road and his car. Fisher crawled forward to watch him go.

.        .        .        .        .

Martineau listened with great interest while Wallace, Fisher and Nash told their story.

'How did Herbie look?' he asked. 'Was he fully dressed?'

'He wasn't dressed at all, sir,' said Wallace. 'A sleeping suit, that's all. No dressing-gown or anything like that. I couldn't tell you if he was wearing slippers.'

Martineau looked at Fisher. 'Are you sure Herbie wasn't in the car when Gabriel set off on the return journey?'

'No, sir. I'm not sure of anything like that,' the man admitted. 'Mind you, I was thinking all the time he was in a grave, and I still think so.'

Martineau nodded. 'But you couldn't find it. I suppose you can take us back to the spot?'

'I can take you to where I saw Gabriel on his way back. But there's no telling how far he carried that body in the dark. I thought he was waiting for daylight. He might have made use of that time to keep on walking further away from the road.'

'If he carried Herbie a mile or so he's made it hard for us. It's awful rough country. Some of those little gullies are ready-made graves. Like slit trenches, they are.'

'Is Gabriel under observation again, sir?'

'Yes. He's back at the caravan, but there's no sign of Herbie. It looks as if we're going to have to search a square mile of moorland to find him.'

'What about dogs?'

'We can try with the dogs. But we'll have to try to pick up Gabriel's scent, not Herbie's. I'm assuming that Herbie was carried, and not dragged.'

'Gabriel looked awful tired, sir.'

'He may be even more tired before the week is out. All right, you men had better go home and get some sleep. I want to see you back here at two o'clock. You did very well.'

130

When he was alone Martineau sat in thought. He decided that it would be better, if possible, to leave Gabriel entirely unaware that his movements during the night had been observed. Which meant that he would have nothing of Gabriel's to provide the dogs with a scent. Without dogs he would need a great number of men. He would also have to inform the West Riding Police that he was going to stage an operation in their territory. Probably they would offer assistance. The whole thing would have to be done without any word of it appearing in the newspapers. Martineau left his office and went along to see Chief Superintendent Clay, the boss of the city C.I.D. Clay would see that the men were provided, and he would ask the Press to co-operate.

The job was coming to the boil very nicely, he felt. There was no self-satisfaction in the thought. He could see great gaps in the framework of his evidence, and the big job, the murder of Ella Bowie, was still a mystery. He was certain that Gabriel and Herbie were somehow involved in it, but his efforts to solve the puzzle were governed by that notion. All possible inquiries in other directions were still being made. Hundreds of people had been interviewed by detectives and hundreds of tips, hints and so-called clues had been checked.

So far as Martineau knew, nothing had happened to make the criminals feel more than normally uneasy. All of them were under the impression that their plans were working out perfectly. But if Herbie's body were found buried, and if Herbie had been murdered, the dream of security would have to be shattered. 'Then,' the chief inspector mused grimly, 'we'll see who cracks first.'

# THIRTEEN

At two o'clock that afternoon, a lot of policemen who would normally have been wearing uniform paraded at 'A' Division Headquarters in plain clothes. A fleet of police vans and cars had been assembled, and the vehicles, packed with men, set off at intervals of two minutes, so that they would attract less attention on the road. Their drivers were instructed to maintain a speed of thirty miles an hour on the open road, and their destination was the spot on the moorland road where Gabriel Lovell had left his car the night before. Detectives Nash and Fisher rode in the first vehicle, with Martineau.

Sergeant Devery and Policewoman Valentine, having a car of their own and no urgent duties, joined in the operation without invitation.

It was a beautiful day for a jaunt in the country. The sun had shone uninterruptedly since dawn, but a cool breeze kept the temperature down. On the moors the men poured out of cars and vans, stretched themselves and looked pleased. They knew what they would be searching for. It was worthwhile police work, and a nice change from patrolling a beat.

Martineau and his immediate aides marshalled them at the roadside in a long line with about four yards between each man. Thus they covered a front of about a quarter of a mile, with the pick-and-shovel detail in the middle. The men knew that they had to keep a good line to ensure an effective search.

With Martineau walking in front of the line like a captain leading an advance, they set off up the hill. Fisher walked near Martineau like a company runner. When the line was

132

poised on a sloping ridge, with the end of the line on the very spot where Gabriel had trudged into view at daybreak, Fisher put his head down like a hound on a trail. It was an attitude well understood. The search was on.

The line went down a long slope, steep at first but easy later. It was the edge of a wide upland valley which seemed to be the main watershed of a distant reservoir. Little groups of sheep could be seen. The reservoir and a few broken drystone walls were the only marks of mankind. The walls were black, and very old. The land was so rough that Martineau wondered why ever they had been built.

The men searched in their various ways. Some walked upright, other stooped peering into narrow gullies. Most of these were a foot or two wide and three or four feet deep, worn into the peat by tiny streams of water.

Martineau had calculated that one mile would be the limit. He did not see how Gabriel could have carried Herbie's body further than that. But before his men had traversed half a mile he began to think about wheeling them to go back on the next quarter-mile of frontage. No doubt Gabriel had more than his share of strength and endurance, but his task, over such country in moonlight, had been one that would have tested a mule.

While Martineau was making up his mind the grave was located. It was found by a recruit called Boon, a rosy-faced lad from the heart of Westmorland, who had been nick-named 'Shepherd of the Hills' by his fellow probationers. Unlike his city-bred colleagues Boon knew how to search in rough country. He had been told to look for a grave, and he did not get excited over a badger hole or a fox's earth, or a little scree of loose peaty soil which had been caused by natural subsidence. He walked upright with his long, slow, hillman's stride and looked for a grave. He did not find it in a gully. He noticed a patch of bilberry about seven feet long and about three feet wide at its widest part. The reddish-green colour of it was right, because it had not yet had time to show the result of disturbance. But Boon, who had seen more bilberry patches than his mates had had good dinners, looked twice at it, then moved directly across to it. Somehow it seemed to him to be a little too humped. Considering the type of country, there was no reason why it should not have been a hump twice as high, but Boon's intuition, born of experience, told him that it was not quite natural. He stooped and rolled back the already uprooted bilberry like a carpet. Beneath, the peaty earth still showed the marks of the tool which had tried to beat it flat.

Boon put his whistle to his mouth, and the shrill blast halted the line. Men did not come a-running. They stayed where they were. Only Martineau and Fisher approached the grave. When he was close to it Martineau signalled to the pick-and-shovel men.

The body was soon uncovered. It was Herbie, lying flat on his back with his arms down at his side, and his feet crossed like a crusader's effigy. His face was composed with closed eyes. There was nothing in the grave but the body in pyjamas, and a hypodermic syringe. Martineau used his handkerchief to pick up the syringe, and then he wrapped it carefully. He did not put it in his pocket, but carried it slung in its wrapping.

'We forgot something,' he said. 'We should have had a stretcher.'

'I think there'll be one in the utility van, sir,' somebody said.

'All right. Two of you nip off and get it. Inspector Williams, please dismiss the parade. Tell them to return to town and resume normal duties.'

By signalling and shouting, Williams made himself understood, and the men trooped back to the road. Martineau began to search the ground around the grave, and those who remained joined in the search. Nobody found anything of note, not even a footmark. 'All right, there is nothing,' the chief inspector said. 'You men can smoke, but put your burnt matches and tab ends in your pockets. The Chief Constable might decide to come out here and look around. He won't like it if the place is littered like a taproom floor.'

Gratefully the men, five in all, lit their cigarettes and found places to sit. They were content: in the midst of great events and allowed to relax for a while. Martineau stood and looked at the grave. It would have to be photographed before it was filled in. Then it would have to be marked. Would it have to be guarded for a day or two? He thought not. He could not see any need for that.

The two men arrived with the stretcher. The body, stiff in *rigor*, was lifted gingerly from the grave. Four men carried the loaded stretcher back to the road. To await the photographers, Boon was left beside the grave, another man in sight of him on the ridge, and another at the roadside.

·    ·    ·    ·    ·

At Headquarters the hypodermic was examined for fingerprints. There were prints, but they were smeared and useless for purposes of identification. Martineau showed no sign of disappointment. He took the syringe with him to the mortuary, where he met a police surgeon and a pathologist from the police forensic laboratory. The pathologist, Dr. Adams, was no carrion-sniffing ghoul. He was pleased to have a body which was, in a manner of speaking, still in the pink of condition.

'What have you got to tell us before we start?' he asked breezily.

Martineau showed him the hypodermic. 'This was in the grave,' he said.

'In relation to what, do you think?'

'Cocaine, possibly.'

'Just cocaine?'

'Cocaine hydrochloride, I think. If there's no cocaine you might look for diamorphine.'

Adams took the hypodermic and looked at it closely. 'If you made the solution strong enough,' he said, 'this thing would hold enough cocaine hydrochloride to kill an elephant.'

'In what?'

135

'In water, plain water.'

'You're the doctor,' said Martineau. 'I'll wait outside.'

'You can wait at your office. I'll phone you.'

'I'll wait outside. I waited in my office once before, and you forgot.'

Dr. Adams laughed with real amusement and no regret. 'Ah, I remember,' he said. 'I went off somewhere for the week-end, didn't I?'

'Fishing in Swaledale,' said Martineau. 'And the pub had no telephone.'

'Ah yes,' said Adams. 'Well, to work!'

Martineau went out, into the comparatively pleasant atmosphere of the mortuary yard.

An hour later Dr. Adams emerged, walked straight past him without seeing him, got into his car and drove away. Martineau sighed. He went and looked into the laboratory, where the surgeon was talking to the attendant.

'Well?' he asked.

The surgeon looked surprised, and then he laughed. 'Didn't he tell you? He's gone to the lab. to make his tests.'

'Cocaine?'

'Yes. Plenty.'

'That the cause of death?'

'Undoubtedly.'

'Could it have been self-administered?'

'It *could* have been, yes.'

'But not likely?'

'I wouldn't say that. It could have been either way.'

'Anything else?'

'No. Perfectly healthy body, run to fat a bit. No marks prior to death, except the jab.'

'Where?'

'Right forearm. An easy place to get at.'

'Thanks,' said Martineau. He went out to his car where Cassidy sat at the wheel. 'Get after Adams,' he said. 'He's floating in a cloud of litmus paper.'

At the laboratory Adams was busy with a test tube and a dropper. When he noticed Martineau he looked surprised until he remembered. 'Ah yes. Won't be a minute,' he said.

Without understanding, Martineau watched diluted chromic acid as it went drop by drop into the test tube. With each drop a precipitate was formed. 'Does that mean cocaine?' he asked, and the scientist nodded.

Martineau waited. He knew that when Adams had done with the job it would be complete, and the evidence he presented would bear the assaults of the bitterest defence counsel.

.      .      .      .      .

The last report from the Dodge City observers assured Martineau that Gabriel was still in his caravan. Martineau went to get Gabriel. He knocked on Gabriel's door, but the knock was not answered. He tried the door and found that it was locked. He bellowed in the name of the law, and silence was the reply.

The Hillman car was there beside the caravan. Its radiator was cold. Obviously Gabriel was at home. Again Martineau knocked and shouted. He succeeded in bringing out the neighbours, but he did not bring out Gabriel.

There is one thing about a door at the head of a little wooden ladder. It is difficult for a man, no matter how powerful and impatient he is, to get his shoulder to it with any effect. Martineau had to send for the keys. He waited stoically. Time was going: time at the mortuary, time at the laboratory, time at Dodge City. As he waited a small fear nagged at him. He didn't see Gabriel as a suicide type, but why didn't he answer? Was he also dead of an elephant-sized dose of cocaine hydrochloride? No, how could he be? He had no hypodermic. Well, he could take the stuff some other way, couldn't he?

Cassidy arrived with the keys. He found one which would fit. They entered the caravan, and with mixed feelings Martineau perceived that it was unoccupied. The place was tidy. Everything appeared to be in order. The one thing out of order was Gabriel's absence.

Martineau looked briefly through the window, in the direction of the store shed on the other side of the factory wall.

'Gabriel slipped out of the door and round the side of the trailer,' he said. 'Those fellows over there must have been taking a gander at a bit of stuff tripping along that road.'

Cassidy remained silent. He felt sorry for the men in the store shed.

## FOURTEEN

SO THE WORD went out for Gabriel Lavengro alias Lovell. It went out into the night because the early spring dusk had turned to darkness. Out of the darkness the word brought Detective Constable Fisher, looking eager and doubtful. Martineau remembered that he had left Fisher standing at the roadside up on the moors, waiting to guide the police photographers to Herbie Small's grave.

'You got back all right then, Fisher?' he said. Naturally he was pleased with Fisher.

'Yes, sir. I wanted to see you about that.'

'Yes?'

'Well, as we were coming back in our car I was on the rear offside, right behind the driver. A bus passed us, going the other way. I just happened to notice it. We'd gone happen another mile and I saw a fellow walking up the hillside, a good way up. I guessed he must have got off that bus, reckoning our time and how far he'd walked. I wondered what he was doing going up there just before dark. There's nobody lives up there that I know of. There's only old quarries, and that.'

'So?'

'Well, sir.' Fisher paused, and now he was in an agony of doubt. There was a chance that he might be starting police action which would make a fool of everybody, with himself the biggest fool of the lot. 'Well, sir,' he began again. 'He was a good way off, but I thought he had a look of Gabriel Lovell. The same sort of action. I've seen him walk the moors, sir, though he was fagged out at the time. I just thought it looked like him, but at the same time I knew—I thought I knew—he was safe under observation in Dodge City.'

'That's interesting,' said Martineau. 'We'll certainly do something about that.'

Fisher swallowed. 'I only *thought* it was him, sir.'

Martineau grinned. 'I know how you feel. You won't be blamed if the man turns out to be somebody else. Go and have a look in the map cupboard. See if you can show me the place.'

Fisher departed. The chief inspector sat in thought. It seemed obvious to him that he would need his best men to trap the gypsy. This time he would not be seeking a dead man in the heather, but one who was almost too much alive. For a start, he began to write down his requirements: three cars with three drivers; then Devery, Ducklin, Cassidy, Cook, Evans, Hearn, Murray. And Fisher. And himself. That would be enough. Whether the men were on duty or off duty, they would come.

Fisher returned with a section of twenty-five-inch ordnance map which showed every field and every permanent structure in the area it covered. 'Here it is, sir,' he said, spreading the map and holding it down on the desk. 'There's this pub on the low side of the road, and then this little farmhouse, and after that there's nothing for miles.'

'And where is the bus-stop?'

'I make it about here, sir. I saw Gabriel climbing up here, and he must have been making for this quarry. There is nothing else.'

'Where there's a quarry there must be a road of some sort. Ah, here it is! It starts much further on, to avoid the hill Gabriel was climbing.'

'That's it, sir. He took the short way on foot. Very likely that would bring him to the top of the quarry face.'

'I wonder if the quarry is still worked.'

'They'll know at the pub, sir. It's called the Nag's Head. They might have a phone.'

'No. The people at the pub might know Gabriel, and they might know he's up there. An inquiry on any pretext about the quarry might ruin everything. If it were merely mentioned to Gabriel he'd know we were after him.'

'Yes, sir. So we leave it severely alone.'

'Yes. I shall want you here an hour before sunrise. That's an order. If you're supposed to be doing something else, tell your sergeant you must have a relief.'

.　　　　.　　　　.　　　　.　　　　.

A big police station never sleeps, but there is a time in the very early morning when it may be said to doze. At that time of day, usually, there is nobody of a higher rank than inspector on the premises, and only one—the inspector in charge of the Night Watch—of that rank. The C.I.D. is closed and dark. The Traffic section has one car and a driver standing by, and a few cars out on Area Patrol. The gaoler on duty has got his prisoners bedded down, having by enforcement of the Ways and Means Act managed to quell the most persistently unruly drunks. The front office staff, having no members of the public to lay complaints, or claim lost property, or ask any of the thousand questions asked in a day's time, are gossiping and smoking over their work. Everybody on duty is simply passing the time, looking for the first hint of grey light which will eventually be followed by the blessed hour of six o'clock, when the Early Turn can have it all, and welcome.

But at four o'clock on the morning of Martineau's second moorland operation there were bright lights in the C.I.D., and a certain amount of bustle. Though there were only twelve men involved, their activities woke up the 'A' Division Station and passed on the time very nicely. When they had gone, home-time seemed to be much closer.

It was yet another fine night, with the promise of another glorious sunrise. The fine weather and the select company gave the expedition the air of an outing. The men were in excellent spirits, and even Martineau had to suppress a certain exuberance. High hopes banished his tiredness. To-day, this coming day, he was going to clear at least one major crime. Fisher's glimpse of Gabriel on the hillside had the hallmark of one of those golden pieces of luck which policemen pray for.

Martineau's briefing was brief indeed, and then the three cars were racing along the empty road to Boyton. It was broad daylight when they sped through that seemingly deserted place, and then they had only six miles to go. Laconic, crime-wise Evans began to quote: ' "As on my trusty charger borne, through sleeping towns I ride . . ." ' He was allowed to go on with that, his mates listening in silent surprise. But when he came to the line ' "My strength is as the strength of ten because my heart is pure" ' there was a howl of derision.

In Boyton the little procession of vehicles was joined by a county police car with two uniformed officers, there, as someone remarked, to see that the city men didn't take a piece of the county with them when they went back to town.

Beyond Boyton the operation began when Devery's car, carrying also Hearn, Cook and the driver, turned left to take the more northerly of two roads. Martineau, with the rest of the party, went along the road which he had travelled the day before. The county car followed Martineau.

Devery's car surged up a long gradient. Beyond its crest the sky was bright. The car went over the crest, and up and over another. The sun appeared, laying long lines of light across the barren countryside. The road took a turn, and on the left the land rose steadily again. On the right, southward, there was a long slope downhill to Martineau's road, but only a section of it was visible to Devery. The rest of it was concealed by the ridge where Gabriel had been seen climbing. Devery could see the north-eastern side of the ridge, and the weathered brown precipice of the quarry which had been cut in its flank.

The colour of the stone showed that the quarry had been abandoned for many years. At the base of the stone face there was a flat sandy area of an acre or so. On one side of this there were three stone huts, and, at some distance in the heather, a much smaller fourth. Devery guessed that they had been the quarry office, storeroom, quarrymen's shelter and, safely remote, the explosives store.

The beams of the rising sun already shone on the upper part of the distant rock face, and with every passing minute the shadowed lower part visibly decreased in size.

When Devery's car reached a point from which he had a good view of the quarry and the surrounding country, he told the driver to stop.

All four men alighted, and inhaled the pure air. Devery stood at gaze, looking for a movement below. There was no question of concealment. A car on that part of the upper road could not be hidden from anybody standing near the quarry.

A car came into sight on the open section of the lower road, and it stopped when its occupants observed Devery's car. The third city police car, with Martineau in charge, would be waiting near the bus-stop where Gabriel had alighted the night before.

Soon the sun's rays were on the sandy floor of the quarry. Its brightness emphasized the dissolute state of the hutments. That brightness also aroused a sleeper. From the largest of the huts a man stepped out of doors. He stretched his arms in the sunshine, and then he put a hand to his face as if he were yawning. Obviously he did not expect to be overlooked at that time of day, out of sight of any habitation. He looked at the sky, then he looked at the land. Watching him, Devery was aware of the exact moment he perceived the cars and men on the northern skyline.

The man, whom Devery assumed to be Gabriel, moved immediately. He ran directly away into the quarry. He ran only a few yards, and then he stopped. Possibly he realized that he could not scale the face of the quarry. He retraced his steps and ran to the south-eastern end of the quarry. There he began to climb the ridge. He climbed rapidly up the steep gradient, but twice he stopped to look back. He must have been puzzled when he saw that Devery and his men had not moved.

He reached the top of the ridge and stopped. He looked down at Martineau's car, then further along the road at the other car, which was Cassidy's, then back at Devery.

Obviously he was measuring distances with his eye, and considering his chances of escape. He had a choice of two directions.

The roads on which the two groups of policemen stood diverged, running to north-east and south-east from Boyton. The further eastward into open country a fugitive ran, the further away from both roads he could be. But he would be under observation from one road or the other for several miles. Only if he succeeded in reaching the height of land, above and away from any road, would he have a chance to escape in that direction.

If, on the other hand, the fugitive ran to the west, he would be between two converging roads which would eventually meet. The further he went in that direction, the more obstacles he would encounter, and the less elbow room he would have. His pursuers would be drawing nearer to him as he went, and there was a possibility that he would run into a dead end.

Devery surmised that Gabriel, the gypsy, would choose to run for open country. He was astonished when Gabriel went over the ridge and plunged out of sight to the west.

Devery's driver ran to the car and began to turn it in the road. When he had done so, he remained at the wheel with the air of a man ready to go, and go fast. 'Hold it a minute,' said Devery. 'This might be a stunt.'

He waited, staring anxiously, but Gabriel did not reappear. He saw Cassidy's car turning to go back, and he dared not wait any longer. Getting into the car he said: 'Don't forget he's on foot. Your speed is ten miles an hour until we get a sight of him.'

'That little farm,' said Hearn when the car was moving. 'Could he get the car out of the barn, or something like that?'

'*I* don't know,' Devery retorted. 'I passed the place twice yesterday, and all I saw was a horse in a field.'

'Yes, up on the hillside,' Cook agreed. 'I saw the horse.'

'Keep your eyes open,' Devery snapped. 'Hearn, you flatten your nose against the back window.'

The car went on, its occupants peering out. For about a mile a change in the unpredictable landscape presented them with a steep bank which blocked their view of the lower land. They were still in this section when a distant cacophony of motor horns came to their ears.

'Stop the car,' Devery said.

They sat in the stationary car, listening. At last there was only one horn, and then it stopped.

'I wonder what all that was about,' the driver said.

Frowning in thought, Devery shook his head. Then he reached for the horn button and held it down. The steady blare of sound floated over the hills. He released the button and waited. He heard a succession of short hoots in reply.

'I think Martineau is trying to tell us to turn back,' he said.

Once more that car was turned round and driven towards its former station at high speed. When the open country and the quarry came in sight, the reason for Martineau's hooting was made clear. Gabriel was coming up the hill towards them, riding a sturdy Galloway pony. He had neither saddle nor bridle, but the little horse seemed to be obeying him willingly. Neck arched and mane flying, it had found some comparatively smooth going, and was coming up the slope at a canter.

'Step on it,' said Devery. 'If he gets across this road we've lost him.'

'How are we going to stop him on a horse?' the driver demanded.

Devery did not know how they were going to stop Gabriel, but he knew that he would have to be stopped. The first requirement was to get in his way.

Gabriel had seen them. When he was a hundred yards from them he brought the horse to a walk. He did not attempt to cross the road but rode parallel with it. Devery saw the white of his teeth as he smiled. The police car had to move at the horse's pace, and Gabriel seemed to have the game in his hands. He could ride steadily along until

Martineau on the other road was miles away, then turn and ride up to the height of land. The policemen would have to follow on foot.

'This is a hell of a do,' said Devery savagely. 'Who ever thought he'd find a bloody horse?'

'I don't know how it let him catch it in a field,' Cook complained. 'It isn't as if it was his own Galloway.'

'He can charm birds, so he wouldn't have much trouble with a horse,' the sergeant rejoined bitterly.

'Car coming up behind,' the driver said with an eye on his mirror.

The car came up at speed. Hearn squinted at the rear window. 'Cassidy,' he said. 'The Guv'nor must have told him to drive round and give us a hand.'

'That's a help,' said Devery. 'He can join the procession.'

That was exactly what Cassidy and his crew did. They crawled along behind Devery, waiting for instructions. The sergeant was wondering whether to send them ahead with orders to leave their car and make for the hilltops, when the landscape made his decision for him.

The land beat Gabriel. There was a little bridge where the road crossed a wide, deep gully. The sides of the gully were perpendicular at the top. Riderless, the pony could have got down into it, but it certainly could not have climbed out at the other side. Gabriel turned and followed the course of the gully, away from the road and down into the wide valley where he had buried his friend Herbie. So much downhill meant so much more uphill before he could reach the highest moors by that route.

Devery signalled to Cassidy, and the Irishman's car drew up alongside. 'You keep crawling along here, just so he doesn't double back,' the sergeant said. 'I'll make for the hilltops to head him off.'

Cassidy acknowledged the order. His car dropped back as Devery's driver put on speed. The road took on a more definite gradient, and the car raced up it to the highest point. Contrarily, the land now sloped away on the northern side of the road, and the higher land was to the south. It was this high land which Gabriel would have to reach to make his escape.

When he saw the road ahead begin to slope down into Yorkshire, Devery told his driver to stop. He, Cook and Hearn alighted, and took to the heather. At the fastest walking pace they could maintain, they made for the highest point they could see. While Gabriel was out of their sight they were uneasy. Now, it did not seem likely that he could reach the height of land before they did, but they wanted to have him in view so that they could be sure.

The climb did not become easier as they toiled upward, and they did not have the consolation of knowing that it would be less easy for the fugitive, because he had a horse. And when they arrived at the place which had seemed to be the highest point, they found that they were at the foot of yet another gradient. But it was an easy one, another of the sloping plateaux which were a feature of the landscape.

Across the uneven tableland Devery could see a mile to the east and nearly two miles to the south. So it was obvious that Gabriel was still down below, hidden by the roll of the land. The sergeant led the way across to the adjacent edge of the plateau. That way he expected to arrive at the top of the steep declivity which he had seen from the road. From that crest he hoped to get a view of the valley with Gabriel in it.

When he reached a place where the land a few yards to his right seemed to fall away sharply, Devery called a halt. Then he went forward at a crouch and finally he crawled. There was a rock which jutted, and he moved along it until he could look down into the valley. Gabriel was still down there in country which was too rough for a rider. He was on foot, leaping from hummock to hummock and striding over gullies, and the pony was following him as best it could.

Devery looked to the south and realized that Martineau would be unsighted and unable to find out what was happening. He would assume that Gabriel was somewhere near the northern road and far along it, when actually he was now nearer the southern road. But he would have that southern road well covered. Gabriel would be seen if he tried to cross it.

Devery moved back a little way in case the keen-eyed gypsy should happen to look upward. 'Grab some greenstuff and hold it in front of your faces, and come and have a look,' he called to Cook and Hearn. They tugged at the tough heather, and then crawled forward.

'He seems to be coming this way,' Hearn remarked.

'Straight up to this spot seems to be the easiest way,' the sergeant agreed. 'If he doesn't see us we have a chance.'

He looked southward again and saw three men as they appeared on the ridge at the other side of the valley. They were spread out in line. They began to move down towards Gabriel. Only if he changed direction did they have any chance of overtaking him. There was no doubt that Gabriel could see them, but he did not appear to be concerned about them.

He reached the foot of the steep, and stopped and looked around for the pony. It was making its way towards him, and he waited for it. It went up to him nodding and tossing its head as if pleased to be with him again. He sprang on to its back and set it at the hill.

When he reached the crest he looked over the tableland, and there was not a soul in sight. He patted the neck of the pony, which was obviously tiring, and urged it forward. Then Hearn leaped up in front of him, from behind a boulder. At Gabriel's shout and spurring action the Galloway also leaped. But Hearn had a grasp of the rider's coat, and from either side Devery and Cook had appeared. Gabriel beat at Hearn's head with his fist, but the tall young man succeeded in improving his hold. He lost his footing, but not his grip. Gabriel was dragged from his seat. He struggled on the ground until he found that he had three assailants.

'All right,' he growled without anger. 'Take it easy, will you?'

## FIFTEEN

DEVERY signalled to the men on the other side of the valley, and then he and his men took the prisoner down to the northern road. Gabriel strolled along between Hearn and Cook, and entertained them. He identified birds for them and whistled down a spiralling skylark. He pointed out the red disappearing brush of a fox which he had espied and they had not. He named moorland flowers for them. He was charming. Hearn kept hold of his arm all the way.

The pony followed Gabriel, occasionally nudging his back. When the party reached the car Devery said to Cook: 'You once told me you wished you were a cowboy. Ride that mustang back to the farm.'

'I only meant a television cowboy,' Cook protested, but he grinned as Devery helped him to mount the pony. 'Giddap,' he said, digging in his heels, and the Galloway began to walk sedately in the right direction.

They drove Gabriel round to the bus stop which was Martineau's station. The remainder of the party was waiting there. The gypsy smiled when he saw the chief inspector. 'Nice morning,' he said.

'I don't remember a nicer,' was the reply. 'I must do this more often. It's done me the world of good.'

'Were you after partridge eggs as well?'

'No, and you weren't either.'

'Oh. What was I looking for?'

'The North Sea, the way you were going. What made you spend the night at the quarry?'

'Just a place to lay my head. There's peace and quiet up here. There *was* peace and quiet.'

'If peace and quiet is all you want, I think I can arrange

for you to have plenty. Hearn, give him one bracelet, and give yourself the other. Go and sit in the back of a car. I want to have a look at the quarry.'

Leaving Gabriel well guarded, the majority of the party went over the ridge to the quarry. When they arrived Martineau detailed men to search the buildings. Devery stared around. 'How do you think he found this place?'

'He may have spotted it on his way in, from the road up there,' Martineau replied. 'Or Badger may have put him on to it. Badger will know about this place, being a gambler. It'll have been surveyed as a possible pitch-and-toss site at some time, and rejected because it's too open on one side. Gabriel was going to use it as a hiding place, or else it was just a stopover for him on his way out. He spotted his surveillance, without a doubt. He did that just too late for his own good, but it would make him wonder how much we'd seen. So he thought he'd get out of the way and leave Badger to keep tabs for him, to let him know if and when it was safe for him to reappear. Of course, when he saw you on the top road this morning, he'd know it was a matter of getting clear away.'

Devery nodded and began to wander away towards the quarry face, but the man in charge called him back. 'What do you think you're going to find in there?' he demanded.

The sergeant explained. When Gabriel had perceived that he was under observation his first action had been to run into the blind alley of the quarry.

'I thought he acted instinctively for a minute,' the sergeant concluded. 'He might have been running to get something hidden there, before he realized that he had better leave it alone.'

Martineau nodded thoughtfully. 'All right, you go in there on your own. You might find footmarks, or something, before the men start tramping around.'

Devery went into the quarry, and the other man sat down on a grassy bank and lit a cigarette. In spite of his belief that the moorland air had been good for him, he was feeling weary. He had been under great strain while

Gabriel was out of sight and, apparently, making his escape.

Before the cigarette was smoked Devery called from the quarry. Martineau found him standing at one side of the sandy quarry bottom. He was among a litter of stone discarded a generation ago, thrown anyhow to be out of the way. He pointed to the ground near a heap of such stone. 'Look,' he said.

'Somebody's been scuffling about here without a doubt,' said Martineau. 'Look, you can see the marks where they've tried to brush away footprints.'

Leaning on the little cairn was a large misshapen slab which tapered from six inches thick to four inches. It looked much too heavy for one man to move. The chief inspector grinned and said to the sergeant: 'Can you move it?'

Devery tried and failed to move the stone. 'You have a go,' he suggested.

Martineau's grin widened. 'A man of my rank doesn't strain his guts lifting stones,' he said. 'Get Evans, he's a Welshman. They're wizards with stones.'

Devery went away and returned with Evans, who looked at the stone as if he were considering the run of the grain.

'Can you move it, Evans?' Martineau asked.

'I can if the sergeant helps me, sir.'

'No. If you can't move it, Cassidy must try. I want to know if one man can do it without help.'

Evans grinned. 'Did you say Cassidy, sir?' He walked around the stone, studying it. He approached it carefully, as if it were alive. Then he crouched beside it and heaved. The stone came up, and he shifted quickly to hold it vertical.

'Told you so,' said Martineau. 'The Celt and the Stone.' Then he fixed his attention on what had been under the stone: something wrapped in a black plastic waterproof.

He moved the waterproof parcel, then scrabbled about with his fingers among loose stones. There did not seem to be anything else hidden there, so he told Evans to let the big stone drop back into its original position.

The three men returned to the grassy bank, where Martineau sat down to unwrap the waterproof. He examined it before he put it aside. It was an ordinary plastic raincoat, and the maker's label had been removed. There did not appear to be any other mark by which it could be traced to an owner. He picked up the object which had been inside the waterproof. It was a brief-case.

It was a good case, of thick, pliant leather, and it had been somebody's property for a long time. On the side of it, beneath the fastener, there had been initials in gilt lettering. These had been mainly erased by some chemical, and there was a whiteish 'tide mark' left by the chemical around the place where the letters had been.

'Stolen, at some time,' Martineau commented. 'Either by Gabriel or Herbie.'

The case was not locked. He opened it. The main compartment held a number of small packages, each neatly labelled as to weight and contents. The labels were clearly printed: 'British Medicaments'.

'Cocaine hydrochloride,' said Martineau. 'Very good. They didn't have time to repack it.'

He counted the packages, laying them carefully on the grass by his side. 'One missing,' he said. 'The one that did for Herbie. Why didn't we find it when we searched? We might have saved Herbie's life.'

'Maybe he had to be killed, drug or no drug,' Devery suggested.

'Maybe. It's a pity. I think he's the one we could have cracked. We'll never crack Gabriel; we'll have to have material evidence.'

'There's enough for murder in one of those little packets.'

Martineau remembered the words of Dr. Adams. 'Enough to kill an elephant,' he said.

He explored the other compartments of the case and came to the conclusion that it had been deliberately emptied before it was used as a receptacle for drugs. Dust and other particles from the case would be analysed at the forensic laboratory, but he did not see how they would be useful in proving ownership. He wanted something more definite than that.

In a fold at the bottom of the case, on the outside, there was the remains of a stick-on label. Even the scraps which had been left were dirty and faded. But by peering at it closely in strong sunlight, with a strong glass and eyes younger than the chief inspector's, Devery was able to read just three letters which had been part of a word.

'T-O-L,' he said.

'Bristol,' Martineau grunted. 'Gabriel pinched it in Bristol.'

He inspected an area of scored leather on the underside of the flap. 'The lad who owned this was careful about his things,' he said. 'He put his own personal mark of identification here, and Gabriel scratched it out. There's just a chance that fluorescence might tell us what it was.'

He returned the packages to the brief-case and closed it. His men seemed to have ended their search of the huts, and they were standing in a group, gossiping. Cassidy came to report that they had found nothing but an unopened bottle of beer, an empty bottle of the same brew and Gabriel's bed. This, he said, had been made of springy bilberry, the plant which had covered Herbie's grave.

Martineau made a short personal inspection of the huts, and then the party returned to their cars. The chief inspector inhaled a last lungful of the moorland air before he took his seat and closed the door of his car. Of one thing he was sure. When he got back to town he was going to eat an enormous breakfast before he did anything else.

.     .     .     .     .

'Now then,' said Martineau. 'Where's Herbie?'

'At the seaside somewhere' Gabriel replied. 'He talked about going to Blackpool. I expect he'll be back in a day or two.'

'Why didn't he take the car?'

'I wanted it myself.'

153

'Did he take any luggage?'

'No. He likes to travel light.'

Martineau met the gypsy's dark gaze. 'He's travelling light, all right,' he said. 'He's on the wing. His body is in the mortuary. We dug him out of his grave the same day you put him in. We found the hypodermic syringe as well. If this morning's little jaunt had taken you a bit nearer to the grave, you would have seen where we've marked it.'

Gabriel received the information with complete impassivity. The brown eyes did not even flicker.

The scene was the interrogation room at Headquarters, a windowless place with bare grey walls and a hard concrete floor. Martineau and Gabriel sat facing each other across a table in the middle of the room, and the contents of Gabriel's pockets were on the table. A single bright light was suspended from the ceiling above the table. At a smaller table in the corner a clerk was taking notes. Devery stood with his back to the closed door.

There was a knock on the door, and Devery opened it to admit Cassidy. The big Irishman handed Martineau a note, and then he stood waiting. The chief inspector read the note and glanced up at Gabriel, who was still coolly watching him.

'It looks as if there's another job coming up,' he said. 'The initials you tried to get off that brief-case were K.L.G. Who was K.L.G?'

Gabriel shrugged. That was all the reply he made.

'We'll try Bristol,' said Martineau. 'I think the case came from there.' He looked at Cassidy and repeated: 'Bristol.' Cassidy nodded and left the room.

'Now give us the truth about Herbie,' Martineau said.

'I don't think he intended to commit suicide,' said Gabriel. 'I think he died of an accidental overdose of a drug.'

'What sort of drug?'

'I haven't any actual knowledge, but he did mention cocaine. He bought the hypodermic and said he was going to have a bash at this main-line stuff to see what it was like. I said: "What are you going to try?" and he said:

154

"Cocaine." I said: "When you get some," and he said: "That's right. When I get some." I don't know when he got it, or if he already had it when he bought the syringe.'

'Was he a sniffer?'

'Not to my knowledge. But he was always after a new sensation. Sort of restless.'

'He's resting all right now. I think you're lying, either wholly or in part, but proceed.'

'Well, I was wakened in the middle of the night by some noise. I'm a light sleeper. Herbie sounded bad, grunting and groaning, and I thought he was having a nightmare. I lit the lamp and saw he looked very queer, and then I saw the syringe on top of his blanket. I guessed he'd had an overdose of something, and I looked and found the mark where he'd taken the needle. I didn't know how to treat him: it was no use making him sick when he hadn't taken the stuff through the mouth. So I got him out to the car and set off to the hospital at Boyton. Before we got to the hospital I found he was dead, so I kept going, and buried him on the moors.'

'Why did you do that?'

'I didn't want the fuss of an inquest. I didn't want the police nosing into my business.'

'I can understand that. What did you use for a shovel?'

'There happened to be an old trenching tool among the stuff in the back of the car.'

'Is it in the car now?'

'No. I threw it away on the moors.'

'After you'd moved Herbie from the trailer to the car, did you go back for anything?'

'Only to turn the light out.'

'You left the light burning.'

'Did I? I must have gone back to shut the door, then.'

'You went inside, and came out carrying something down at your side.'

'Ah, I remember. It was the hypodermic. I thought I'd better take it to the hospital with me.'

'You're lying, aren't you?'

'No. I'm telling the truth.'

'We searched Herbie and we searched you, and we searched the trailer, but we didn't find any cocaine. Where was that single packet hidden?'

'I don't know what you're talking about.'

'Don't you?' Martineau felt in his pocket for cigarettes, and offered the packet to Gabriel. The gypsy accepted a cigarette, put it in his mouth and waited for a light. Martineau was vaguely astonished. There was a lighter lying on the table among Gabriel's personal property. He picked it up himself and thumbed it. There was a good spark but no flame.

'It must have run out of fuel,' said Gabriel.

Martineau's eyes narrowed. He looked at the matchbox which was also lying on the table. He picked it up and found that it contained only three matches.

'How do you mean it *must* have run out of fuel?' he demanded. 'You *knew* it was out of fuel. You've used nearly a box of matches.'

'I carry matches to light the lamp in the trailer,' said Gabriel quickly.

But his explanation came too late. Martineau had picked up a halfpenny from among the loose change on the table, and he was unscrewing the filler cap of the lighter. Gabriel was quite still as he watched.

Martineau peered into the filler hole. 'There's no cotton wool in it!' he exclaimed.

He held the lighter upright and knocked it gently on the table. A few—just two or three—very fine colourless crystals appeared on the smooth woodwork.

'So that's where Herbie hid the stuff,' said Gabriel.

'In your lighter?' asked Martineau with sarcasm.

'It's Herbie's lighter.'

'I doubt it,' was the reply. 'Herbie had no lighter when he was searched last Saturday night. You *did* have a lighter of that type. I'll go on oath about that. The laboratory boys will wash out this lighter and find enough evidence. You murdered Herbie all right.'

'I did not,' Gabriel replied. 'He worked that syringe himself, and you can't prove otherwise.'

'I won't attempt to prove that specifically,' said Martineau. 'I'll just prove beyond any reasonable doubt that you committed murder. You persuaded Herbie to buy the hypodermic on your behalf. I don't know what reason you gave him for wanting it, but I might find out. You wanted rid of Herbie for several reasons. First, he was nervous and showed signs of cracking. We can prove that by his movements. Second, you wanted his share. Third, he had served his purpose and he knew too much: not about robbery, in which he was fully involved, but about murder, in which he was involved only slightly or not at all. So you murdered him. You did not have an entrenching tool in the car, and I think I can prove there was no such tool in the car last Saturday night. You never had any intention of taking Herbie to hospital. After you put him in the car you went back to the trailer and got the little shovel you use for putting coke into the stove. Somewhere on that shovel, just where it joins the handle, I think we'll find particles of peaty soil. Before Herbie was dead you started off from your trailer with the intention of burying him. You intended to murder him and that was your intention before you hid the bulk of the cocaine up at the quarry. You abstracted one packet for Herbie.'

Gabriel was silent.

'I don't need a statement from you about that. I'll go to court without one,' Martineau continued. 'What I do need is a statement about the murder of Ella Bowie. How did you work that? Who did it for you? And who did the key-stealing job for you? If your brother wasn't safe inside I'd say it was him. Have you a cousin?'

'I have a number of cousins,' said Gabriel, 'and I don't know what you're talking about. I knew nothing about Ella Bowie. I never spoke to her in my life, except to order a drink.'

'You knew enough about her to be windy when she happened to see you in the company of that cousin who is so much like you. You thought she might mention the likeness to a policeman who would put two and two together. You thought it would be better to quieten her, quickly. Then you staged that drunk-in-charge-of-a-car effort to distract attention and give yourself an alibi. That poor girl was murdered just because she happened to tumble to the secret of your miserable double act.'

'That's a lot of nonsense,' said Gabriel.

'Is it? Listen. The cocaine we found ties you to the B.M. job, and we'll have another tie when we've talked to certain associates of yours. The B.M. job is tied to the rape of Miss Naylor, by reason of the key which was stolen. That job was done by you and your double. Your drunk-driver effort was timed perfectly to alibi you for the murder. There was no other reason for you to stage that little act. The murder was happening while that went on, and you knew it. Why else would you risk drawing police attention to yourself when the police didn't know you from Adam and might never have picked you up at all? Only in a very serious emergency would you do that, and the emergency was murder. You needed the best alibi you could get, and you took a chance on being suspected of rape and robbery—for which you had an alibi—in order to be damned sure you wouldn't be charged with murder.'

Gabriel lost enough of his steely control to indulge in a sneer. 'You've got it all weighed up, haven't you?' he said. 'And it's all a lot of blah.'

Martineau did not lose his equanimity. Had he done so he would have knocked the prisoner off his chair.

'I'm going to convict you of murder, and of accessory to murder, and of warehouse-breaking,' he said. 'There may be other items as well. You can go and sit in a cell and enjoy yourself figuring how I'm going to do it.'

## SIXTEEN

With Gabriel Lovell in custody, and the news of Herbie Small's murder about to erupt in headlines, it was not advisable to leave Thomas Tiffany and Lewis Badger at liberty. As soon as Tiffany had sent his supposedly drug-laden bales of silk to the docks, he was arrested. Badger, against whom there was no evidence, but a lot of suspicion, was brought in for questioning. Badger sat under escort in the C.I.D. office. He was allowed to see Tiffany being taken into the interrogation room, and he also saw the packages of recovered heroin as they were taken in. But Tiffany did not see him: no signal was passed between the two men.

The packages were on the table at Martineau's elbow when he started his inquisition. Tiffany tried to pretend that they were not there, but Martineau drew his attention to them.

'Yes,' he said. 'You recognize them, don't you? We found them at your place in Abel Street the night before last.'

Tiffany stared. 'You were in there?'

'Yes. With a search warrant, of course. We got this stuff and marked it before we brought it away. We did your parcels up again nicely, didn't we? I bet you never noticed they'd been touched.'

There was only the owlish stare by way of reply. It was as much as Martineau expected, so early in the interview. He was accustomed to suspects playing for time while they made up their minds whether to put up a defence or remain silent.

'You have been told that you need not make a statement unless you wish to do so,' the policeman went on. 'This is

one of the times when we don't give a damn what you do.
We've got you right. Whether you speak or not makes no
difference to us.'

'What led you to my place?'

'A friend of yours.'

'Badger?'

Martineau shrugged and smiled. 'We don't disclose the
names of our informants.'

'Badger wouldn't give anything away,' said Tiffany, but
there was doubt in his voice.

'And Gabriel wouldn't, would he? It makes you wonder
who could have done.'

'Gabriel?'

'Oh yes. He's down in the cells.'

Tiffany thought about that. Martineau watched him and
then said: 'It wasn't Herbie who coughed. He never said
a word. And never will.'

'It sounds like Herbie, you defending him.'

'No, you're wrong. He needs no defending. He's out of
our reach.'

'What do you mean?'

'He's dead. Gabriel murdered him.'

'Oh Jesus.' Tiffany was appalled. He did not doubt
Martineau's statement. Nor did he ask *why* Herbie had been
murdered. He knew Gabriel, and he was perhaps less
shocked by the news of Herbie's death than by the thought
that it might have been the death of some other member of
the gang. Himself, for example.

'I should have retired years ago,' he said regretfully. 'It
isn't as if I couldn't have afforded it.'

'It's been going on for years, has it?'

'I haven't said anything about anything going on, have
I? I just said I should have retired.'

'I'm sure you're right. Wouldn't they let you retire?'

'Nobody stops me from doing what I want.'

'I dare say somebody will for the next few years. What do
you drink? Whisky? There'll be no more whisky for a long,
long time.'

160

Tiffany looked at a future without whisky, and was even more appalled. His dismay was pitiful, but he was in the hands of men who could have no pity for a smeck merchant in any circumstances. Dealers in drugs for the ruination of mankind were not regarded as ordinary criminals. Martineau himself, through long experience of malefactors, could be tolerant of all but the worst. This man, Tiffany, was of the worst. The chief inspector perceived his condition and sought to exploit it, concealing a ruthless purpose with bland words.

'You don't look as fit as you might be,' he said. 'It's hard lines when a man like you has to go inside for a long stretch. When a man is no longer young he's liable to die doing time. Unless he's as strong as a horse.'

'I'm not as strong as a horse and never was. I want to do the best I can for myself.'

'There isn't much you *can* do. *I* can't make a deal with you. Nobody can. But if your attitude and actions showed you were forced into things, by threats or blackmail, you *might* get a lighter sentence.'

'And suppose the judge wouldn't believe me?'

Martineau shrugged. 'You'd have to back your story by your actions. Constructive repentance.'

'You mean I'd have to cough up the lot?'

'Indeed, yes.'

'I needn't. I could still be in fear.'

'Oh, sure. Tell the judge you were frightened, and daren't say who frightened you. You could try that. It *never* works.'

'Well, you seem to have got everybody, already.'

'Everybody?'

'This is one case you're dealing with. All the evidence will relate to one particular consignment, not some other consignment at some other time. The judge will stick to this one job. If he wants to know where the stuff came from you can tell him. No suppliers are involved. If you or the judge want to know about regular suppliers you're being irrelevant to the issue. I can't tell you, anyway. This is the first time I've been mixed up in anything of the sort.'

Martineau grinned ruefully. He realized that Tiffany was more intelligent than he had thought. Pressure could not be applied to gain evidence of a regular drug traffic in one single case where the drug had been stolen. There was suspicion concerning a regular traffic, but no evidence at all.

'There is a regular supplier, all the same,' he said. 'You can't show true repentance without assisting the police in their inquiries about that.'

'You heard what I said. This is the first time for me.'

'All right. That's your story. It won't do you any good. Long time no whisky.'

'If I tell all I know about this case you can't grumble.'

'Tell it, then.'

'What do I get if I do?'

'Time.'

'No leniency?'

'You might get a bit of leniency from me, but I'm only a police witness. If the defence intimates that you have been of assistance to the police, I might not deny it.'

'Oh, to hell with you,' said Tiffany.

Martineau smiled and waited. Now, all he hoped to get from Tiffany was information which would lead to the obtaining of evidence against Badger, if Badger had been illegally active in the case.

Tiffany thought awhile, then said suddenly: 'Which of 'em shopped me?'

'You know I can't tell you that.'

'If I thought it was Badger . . . You can tell me this, did he have *anything* to do with it?'

'Yes, he had something to do with it.'

'Did *Gabriel* have anything to do with it?'

'No, only very indirectly.'

'So it was Badger. I'll fix him up. Can I trust you not to tell him it was me?'

'I won't involve you if I can avoid it.'

'Well, he's the regular contact with London. You'll be searching his place, anyway, so you can find your evidence without seeming to have been told. Somewhere in his room you'll find an ordinary ready reckoner. It won't be hid. There's about half a dozen pages in the whole book with marks against certain numbers. It's some sort of a code. It's his address book and record book.'

'Thanks. We should be able to crack the code if it's one of those numbers-for-letters things. Nobody will ever know you told me about it. Is he the paymaster?'

'Locally, you mean? I'm not telling you anything about that.'

'I'm assuming he is. How did Gabriel come to be connected with him?'

'Gabriel was sent here. Don't ask me who sent him or why. He's worked all up and down the country, has Gabriel. That caravan of his is real handy.'

'Did Badger do the scouting on the B.M. job for Gabriel and Herbie?'

'That I cannot tell you. I knew nothing about that business, and didn't want to know.'

'You saw the labels on these packets, didn't you?'

'No business of mine. They could have put 'em on a-purpose, for all I know.'

'Why would they do that?'

'Well, wide boys get up to all sorts of gags, don't they?'

'You've met Gabriel, I suppose?'

'I met him and Herbie, just once. We had a drink together, that's all. It was just so we'd all know each other by sight. Gabriel's business had nothing to do with me.'

'If Gabriel's business had nothing to do with you why did you have to know each other?'

'Well, happen I said it wrong. We just met socially.'

'Did you? Did you ever meet *Sastreria Enrique Morales* socially?'

For the first time, Tiffany smiled. '*Sastreria* means a tailor's shop,' he said.

'I see. The tailor's shop of Enrique Morales. Do you know Spanish?'

'No. But I know that much.'

'Congratulations. So you just met Gabriel socially. Did you ever meet Ella Bowie socially?'

'What?'

'Who murdered Ella Bowie?'

'Here, hold on a minute!' Tiffany was alarmed. 'Don't get me mixed up in that.'

'You know who did it.'

'No, I don't. Nobody told me, and I never asked.'

'Does Badger know?'

'If you want to know what Badger knows you'd better ask him.'

Martineau sat back in his chair. 'I shall probably want to talk to you again, but for the time being you can go and cool off. Take him away, Sergeant.'

.        .        .        .        .

After the interview with Tiffany, Martineau's first action was to send a messenger to the men who were searching Badger's room, to inform them of the importance of finding and impounding the ready reckoner. 'If they've already found it, bring it back with you,' he told the messenger.

There was also the note of a telephone message from Bristol. The initials K.L.G. appeared to stand for Knight Lancelot Green, a name so unusual that it had been remembered for seven years by a Bristol detective. Knight Lancelot was an accountant employed by a small firm which made covers for car seats. Seven years before, he had been a clerk with the same firm, and at that time he had been studying accountancy. The tell-tale brief-case, his own property, he had used for the purpose of carrying textbooks and homework between home and the office. But on the night of the firm's annual dinner he had eschewed homework and left his case and books at the office. In the office safe, that night, there had also been a week's payroll of the firm, a little under two thousand pounds made up in separate wage packets. Thieves had broken in that evening, ripped the back off the safe, abstracted the wage packets and carried them away in Knight Lancelot's brief-case. Now, Bristol detectives were on their way to talk to Gabriel about the robbery, and they were bringing Knight Lancelot with them, to identify the case.

'Note the timing of that job,' said Martineau. 'The annual dinner. Nobody working late or calling at the office for anything. That's typical of Gabriel's casing.'

'But why keep the brief-case?' Devery wanted to know.

'That's typical too. It's worth a few quid, isn't it? Look how he kept that lighter instead of losing it on the moors. It'll convict him of murder, but it's also worth about thirty bob. Gabriel doesn't throw thirty bob away. The inconsistencies of the criminal mind, my boy. It's a wonder he didn't try to sell the hypodermic back to the chemist.'

'He played right into our hands with that lighter.'

'Yes. It must be a gypsy characteristic, that reluctance to throw useful things away.' Martineau looked at his watch and observed that it was lunch-time. 'There's a razor still hidden somewhere, I feel sure,' he said. 'If we can find it, it might help somewhat in clearing Ella's job.'

'That's a puzzle, that is. I can't figure it at all.'

'Nor can I. When your girl friend comes on duty this afternoon you might go and have another look at the caravan. A real good look. Take an extra man with you if you can find one who isn't busy. There might be something in the caravan.'

'I'll do that, sir,' said Devery. He glanced through the open doorway of Martineau's office, into the main office where Badger was still sitting. The man looked dejected and apprehensive. The busy coming and going of young men, the hurried telephone calls, the brief esoteric remarks which seemed to be sinister jests, the feverish searching of files following sudden ideas, these were activities calculated to make a suspect feel lonely and uneasy. Badger had no notion of what was going to happen to him. He had seen Tiffany taken into Martineau's office, and then taken away to the cells. He assumed that Tiffany's parcel of silk had been opened at the docks, and the drug discovered. That explained Tiffany's presence. But how did it explain his own, unless somebody had been singing a song to Martineau?

Badger was asking himself how much the police knew. How much had they been told and how much had they found out? Had they known about Tiffany's activities for some time, or had they known only for a few hours? Of only one thing was he sure. *He* had given nothing away to the police, he was sure of that.

Looking at him Devery asked: 'When are you going to tackle that fellow?'

'When I've had a look at his ready reckoner, maybe,' said Martineau. 'He's all right. If we leave him long enough he'll have so many tales ready he'll be bound to tell us something.'

## SEVENTEEN

THAT afternoon Devery and Rosamund picked up Bill
Hearn to assist them in the search of the caravan. Because
it was Friday they went to draw their pay, and then they
set off for Dodge City. When they arrived, they left the
Jaguar in the main road and walked through the squatters'
village to the caravan. Devery got to work with the keys,
and opened the door with them in less time than Cassidy
had done. Before he entered, he glanced at the factory
across the way, and saw that he was being watched from
the store shed. Martineau was still keeping the caravan
under observation, or else he had forgotten to withdraw
the observers.

Inside the caravan the three officers started a systematic
search. Rosamund looked in drawers and cupboards,
Devery examined upholstery and bedding, Hearn con-
centrated on the walls and ceiling. He would search the
floor when, eventually, he was compelled to get down to it.

Devery also had something else in mind. It had caused
him to approach Dodge City carefully, and look to left
and right as he walked through it. He hated to leave a job
half-cleared, and he had hoped for a glimpse of a red-
head. The recovered cycle had been claimed, and the time
and place of the theft were known. All that the sergeant
required now was to lay his hands on the thief. It was no
case comparable to the one upon which he was engaged,
but by normal police standards it would be a good little
job if he could catch the bicycle thief. Other cycles had
been stolen in the city. One thief, caught 'right', might
well confess to having stolen a dozen.

Devery's feeling about this took him occasionally to the
door, to look out. He was assailed by a slight regret that

he had not, several days ago, told the observers in the store shed to look out for the red-head. They might have been able to watch the boy's movements, and they might even have seen where he lived. It was too late now, he supposed. The observers would soon be withdrawn.

It was with some such thoughts that he looked out—and saw the red-head. His exclamation caused the others to pause and look up. As he jumped from the doorstep to the ground they ran to the door to see what was the matter. Hearn looked over Rosamund's shoulder and saw the shock of ginger hair disappearing among the caravans, with Devery in pursuit, and he acted impulsively according to what he considered to be his duty. He pushed Rosamund aside and joined in the chase, bearing off towards the centre of Dodge City in the shrewd expectation that the fugitive would soon have to turn in that direction or be forced into the open.

Left alone, Rosamund continued the search. She had not noticed that the caravan was still under observation from the store shed, but she was quite at ease. The door was open, Herbie was in the mortuary and Gabriel was in a police cell, and in any case Devery or Hearn would soon be returning. She worked diligently, hoping to find something of importance—the razor, perhaps—before the others rejoined her. She lifted out drawers and looked for false bottoms and hidden compartments. She unfolded and neatly refolded every article of masculine underwear. Her dainty nose twitched in repugnance as she fished among dirty washing.

She was at the rear end of the long, narrow interior when a small metallic sound made her stop work and turn to look at the open doorway. She could see nobody. She frowned, and then her eyes widened in amazement as the piece of carpet covering the middle of the caravan floor rose up in a way which seemed magical. Its silent movement seemed to portend danger. Fear clutched at Rosamund, and held her rigid. The carpet fell back to disclose a raised trap-door, then the back of a man's head and his broad shoulders appeared. As he climbed clear of the trap-door he lowered it quietly into position, then he strode to the door and closed it. He turned with an expectant grin and Rosamund saw Gabriel Lovell, or the living image of him.

The man's jaw dropped in surprise. 'What are *you* doing here?' he demanded bluntly. As an afterthought he added sternly: 'Women aren't allowed in here. We're dead against it.'

Rosamund had to remind herself that she was a policewoman. She had to appear to be bold to prevent herself from becoming a bundle of useless apprehension.'

'You know what I'm doing here.'

His glinting eyes narrowed as he studied her. 'Where is . . . ?' he began, and stopped. 'How did you get in?'

Rosamund realized that the man did not know her. But Gabriel knew her. He had seen her in the police station on Saturday night, and elsewhere too, probably. This was Gabriel escaped, and now putting on an act for some reason, or else it was not Gabriel. If it was not Gabriel, it was the mysterious cousin or brother who had committed the outrage on Miss Naylor.

'I got in with a key and a search warrant,' she said. 'I'm a policewoman, and I have a perfect right to be here.'

'A policewoman?' He was amused. 'They're improving a bit, I think. Did you come on your own?'

'I came with Sergeant Devery and Constable Hearn.'

'And where are they now?'

'They stepped out. They're just outside,' Rosamund replied, rather breathlessly in spite of her determination to be self-possessed.

'Oh, are they?' The man turned and went to the door, and locked it. Rosamund looked around for a weapon. There was not much which was moveable. She opened a drawer which she had searched only a few minutes before, and picked up a kitchen knife. She was aware of danger, horrid danger, and her confidence ebbed rapidly.

The man returned to face her. He did not seem surprised to see her with a knife in her hand. She saw the strange light in his eyes. This was the one who looked as if he took drugs! The one Miss Naylor had talked about! Oh dear!

'Where's your search warrant?' he asked calmly.

'Sergeant Devery has it.'

'Ah. I don't see why I should believe this tale of yours. No search warrant, no Sergeant Devery. You're a trespasser. I think you came here to steal. The last person you want to see is a copper.'

'There are two of them just outside, I tell you.'

'I never saw anybody outside. What are they doing outside, anyway, if they have a search warrant for inside?'

'They ran after a boy who stole a bicycle.'

'I see. But you said they were just outside. Somebody here is a bit daft, and it isn't me.'

'It's true. They'll be here any minute.'

He grinned. 'You're a nice-looking chick. I bet you'd be worth it.'

'No, I wouldn't, I wouldn't. No girl would be worth what they'd do to you for laying hands on a policewoman.'

'What they'd do if they caught me, you mean. Then if they caught me they'd have to prove it was me. That might be awful hard to prove.'

'Not this time, it wouldn't. Gabriel is in a police cell.'

His smile fled. 'He's what?'

'He's been locked up for murder. He murdered Herbie.'

'What for?'

'I don't know.'

'I don't believe it. You're just trying to put me off.'

'I'm not. It's true,' she cried, frantic in her effort to do exactly what he accused her of doing. She was trying to gain time. Surely either Devery or Hearn would come soon.

'Is that what you're here for, looking for evidence against Gabriel?'

She could see the anger rising in him. 'Just looking for evidence,' she said.

'Against Gabriel?'

'Against anybody.'

'You little bitch,' he snarled, and his rage terrified her.

170

He reached for her. She did not have the killer instinct, and she did not want to kill. Instead of thrusting with the knife, she slashed at his hand. As he withdrew the hand involuntarily, she dodged under his arm and made for the door. He caught her at the door; dragged her away from it and flung her down. Her knife skittered away somewhere. He pounced, but she had rolled with the automatic promptness ensured by training, and she was able to kick him in the stomach. He recoiled, but was up in a moment. She also was on her feet, beside the knife drawer. She pulled out the drawer, and swung it, and he covered his face with his arms as knives, forks, spoons and small kitchen utensils flew in his direction. Then she was at a window, ramming the empty drawer against it. Glass tinkled on the hard ground outside. She hit him with the empty drawer as he dragged her away.

'You little bitch,' he repeated as he took the drawer and threw it down. But this time there was surprise and a certain admiration in his voice. He forced her back against a bunk, using his hands and one knee. He plucked her off her feet and laid her on the floor, his knee grinding painfully into her abdomen. She got her hand to the police whistle in her pocket, and put it to her mouth. She blew one long blast before it was knocked away and torn from her grasp.

The next few moments never became clear in her memory. She struggled with a powerful animal, and with a sense of futility. Though she was frantic with horror and sick with loathing, something in her nature was telling her that she might as well give up the fight. That enemy she did manage to defeat. Since the only alternative was to succumb, she resisted, and while she resisted she became vaguely aware of a pounding and a shouting. Then there were great crashes against the door as someone continued to throw himself bodily at it.

Because of the steps the man outside could not break down the door. But the uproar he made caused Rosamund to find enough strength to scream for help. All this tended to weaken the maniac resolve of her assailant. It worried

171

him. He may have felt that his way of escape was in danger. 'I oughter throttle you,' he growled, and left her. The trap-door closed quietly, and he was gone.

Rosamund lay thankfully getting her breath, then she got wearily to her feet and went to open the door. She looked at the heated and concerned faces of two plain-clothes men from a suburban division, called in to help with 'A' Division's troubles. They stared at her, and peered past her into the caravan with blank bewilderment.

'He came in through the trap-door in the floor,' she explained. 'He went out that way.'

'Who?'

There was no time to explain. 'Big handsome gypsy, just like Gabriel Lovell,' she said. 'Get him if you can. He's worth a fortune to anybody who needs some promotion.'

They were away, stooping to look under the caravan. 'He must have crawled out of the bushes,' one of them said excitedly. They thrashed among the elderberries, then ran off in the direction they hoped the man had taken.

Rosamund sat on the steps of the caravan and trembled. She knew that she ought to go and find a telephone, but she did not have the strength. She reached into the caravan, to where she had put her handbag near the door, and extracted a cigarette and her lighter. She smoked the cigarette, then rose to her feet and dusted her grey suit with her hands. The hands themselves were no longer clean. She straightened the ruins of her stockings, looked at her face in her compact mirror and decided that cosmetic repairs could wait, straightened the little green cap she was wearing, and set off to walk through Dodge City to the Jaguar.

On the way a few people looked at her, but incuriously. Dodge City was used to all types. They did not know that she was a young woman who had narrowly escaped rape or death, or both. Had they known, they would not have been particularly horrified about the rape part.

In the main road, the Jaguar was not in sight. So it seemed that Devery and Hearn had caught the red-headed boy and taken him to Headquarters. 'Silly idiots,' she thought, with the indignation of one who has narrowly escaped injury through another's negligence, 'they missed the chance of a lifetime.'

She walked along the road to a public telephone box. In the box she was compelled to dial nine-nine-nine because she did not have enough pennies for an ordinary call. To the operator at Headquarters she put the question: 'Has Gabriel Lovell escaped from police custody, by any chance?'

'Not that I know of,' the operator replied.

'Then you'd better put me through to Chief Inspector Martineau,' she said. 'And it's urgent.'

It was not Martineau, but a clerk who answered from the C.I.D. 'The chief inspector is engaged at the moment,' he said. 'Can I help?'

'Yes. Disengage him, whatever he's doing. He'll be mad at you if you don't.'

'Real hot, is it?'

'Boiling.'

'Right. Hold the line.'

Presently Martineau announced himself, not irritably, but expectantly. 'Who is speaking?' he asked.

'Policewoman Valentine, sir. The one who is teamed up with Sergeant Devery.'

'Ah yes. And?'

'If you still have Gabriel Lovell under lock and key, I've just seen his double.'

'Where?'

'Dodge City, at Gabriel's caravan.'

'When?'

'About fifteen minutes ago.'

'Where are the men who are supposed to be watching the caravan?'

'They went off after this man.'

'I see. And where is Sergeant Devery?'

'He and Constable Hearn went off after a suspect.'

'What sort of a suspect?'

'A bicycle thief.'

'Ah. Tell me exactly what happened.'

Rosamund told him. In the telling she made sure he understood that the defence of her honour had been successful.

'Oh dear,' he said with sympathy. 'How do you feel now?'

'A bit shaky. But I'll be all right.'

'I'd better send a car for you.'

'No, sir. Please. If I were a man you'd want me to stay on the job. I'm not really hurt.'

'You're quite sure?'

'Yes. I'll be perfectly all right.'

'What are you going to do now?'

'Return to the caravan and continue the search.'

Martineau laughed. 'That's the spirit,' he said. 'Good girl. You'll soon have some help out there.'

But he was not laughing when he put down the receiver. Rosamund's modest phrases had told him how near to serious injury she had been. Devery would have something to be sorry about, he thought. He turned his attention to the organization of the hunt for Gabriel Lovell's spit and image.

Rosamund went back to the caravan. The observers had not yet returned from their hunt for Gabriel's double. While she was still alone, she found that she had a great reluctance to go into the caravan. She sat on the doorstep awhile, and smoked another cigarette. Then she arose, and looked under the caravan at the rear.

There was an old waterproof sheet lying on the ground under the caravan, from the region of the trap-door to the rear end. Also, the axle had a temporary wrapping of canvas. With the caravan backed against the elderberry bushes it had been possible for the third man of Gabriel's company to come and go undetected, without soiling his hands and clothes too much. In this matter Gabriel had hoodwinked the police. Rosamund learned later that the trap-door had been discovered during the first search of the caravan, but its significance in connection with the bushes had not been appreciated.

She searched among the bushes, but she could find no signs of the recent burial of a small object. Since her suit was already thoroughly creased, she did not think she would ruin its appearance further by going under the caravan. She crawled along the groundsheet, feeling for a convexity where something might be hidden. It was her intention to roll up the sheet on her return journey, so that she could examine the ground beneath.

When she reached the axle she looked hopefully at the canvas which covered it. The stuff was loosely wrapped several times round the metal, and held by a few windings of cord. Rosamund slid her hand among the folds at the edge. She searched for some little time in this way, and eventually her fingers closed on a narrow object of wood. She thought at first that it was the handle of a big knife, but when she withdrew it she saw that it was a case for a single razor, a case of the type with a detachable cap. She pulled off the cap, and allowed the razor to slide part of the way out. Elated, she pushed it back and replaced the cap. She did not doubt that this was the razor's usual hiding place. The man who was Gabriel's double had not had time to take it with him when he fled, or he had forgotten it. He had not troubled to pick it up as he came in, and that had been a good thing for Rosamund. She reflected quite coolly—proof that she was getting over her shock— that her sweet neck might have been in two parts if the man had had his razor.

She searched further among the folds of canvas, but found nothing else. She could have gone forward and raised the trap-door, but her nerves were not sufficiently improved to make her want to enter the caravan again. Holding the razor case in her hand, she moved in reverse the way she had come. As her small round behind backed out into the bushes, she became aware of feet on each side of her: two pairs of brown shoes, and the beginnings of two pairs of the lightweight tweed trousers which were currently popular.

She looked up, and was relieved to see Hearn, and

Hearn's face wore a wry grin. She looked the other way and saw Devery. It was the first time she had ever seen him really angry. His face was so grim that she was afraid. But he reached out and helped her to her feet.

'That the razor?' he asked.

'I—I think so. It *is* a razor.'

'So you finished the job off proper, eh?'

She stared at him. Was this professional rancour? Was he going to try and blame her for happening to meet Gabriel's badly wanted double? For giving the story to Martineau? For finding the razor?

'When we've wrapped up here,' Devery said, 'you can drive me to see a psychiatrist. I'll have my head examined.'

She turned pink with relief, and with a feeling which was in the nature of affection. His anger was directed at himself.

'I've been kicking myself,' he said. 'I've been as worried as hell about you. But I see you're all right.'

She nodded, not being able to speak at that moment. She was just realizing that she had a regard for the sergeant which was not entirely professional.

'Would we have got him if we'd been there?' he asked.

'I'm sure you would. He climbed straight into the caravan without looking round.'

'Damn and blast,' he said. 'Never mind. You're unharmed, that's the thing. Due to the foresight of Mr. Martineau, and *not* to the efforts of Mr. Devery.'

She dimpled. 'Never mind, dear. You might get another chance to save me some other time.'

'Tchah!' he said, but he grinned.

'Have they caught the man?' she wanted to know.

'Not yet. He got away.'

'Who is he?'

Devery's grin widened. 'Martineau is trying to find out,' he said. 'I think somebody will be holding a very hot telephone at this moment.'

## EIGHTEEN

IN THE MATTER of discovering the identity of the man
who had attacked Policewoman Valentine, the first step
was to make sure that Lucifer Lavengro was still safely
held at Lambham Hall Criminal Mental Institution. So
Chief Inspector Martineau asked the switchboard to put
him in telephone contact with Lambham Hall, and when
this was done he asked to speak to the Senior Almoner.

'I'm afraid Miss Giles is not available at the moment,'
he was told when he had announced himself. 'She's not
well, and she's in her room.'

'To whom am I speaking?'

'I'm Miss Armstrong, the Junior Almoner.'

'Very well. I'm making inquiries about a patient of
yours called Lucifer Lavengro.'

'He's not here,' said Miss Armstrong frankly. She had
the lilt of youth in her voice, and she seemed to be an
entirely different type to the Miss Giles who had made
Martineau so angry.

'Do you mean he's escaped?'

'No, of course not. But there's been a mistake. I think
that's what is upsetting Miss Giles. She's worrying about the
poor man.'

'Oh, she is, is she? May I ask why?'

'Yes. You see, he'll have nobody to look after him. We
were thinking of getting in touch with the police about it.'

'Why won't he have anyone to look after him?'

'He's been allowed to go to his brother at week-ends,
but earlier this week there was a letter telling us not to let
him go until further notice. His brother will be away for
some time, you see. The letter was mislaid, and it wasn't

177

found until after Lucifer had been let out this morning. Miss Giles is really worried.'

'We'll try and find him,' said Martineau, very mildly.

'Oh, thank you so much.'

'Lucifer stayed with his brother *last* week-end, then?'

'I think so. Just a moment.' There was a long pause. 'Yes,' the girl said. 'He was on leave last week-end. He left on Friday morning and returned on Sunday afternoon before dark.'

'Are those the usual times of departure and return?'

'Yes. None of the patients have let us down yet. Lucifer is *very* conscientious.'

'Mmmm.' Martineau was curious, and he was in no hurry. The more information he had the better. 'How many patients do you let out at one time?'

'I'm sorry. We don't communicate that information.'

'Well, many or few?'

'Few. Now that you know about Lucifer, I may as well tell you. There are only five on the list.'

'Only five trusted inmates, and Lucifer is one of them?'

'That's right. He's rather regarded as Miss Giles's special protégé.'

'I see. How long has this week-end leave business been going on?'

'It was started last summer, and stopped for the winter. The week before last it was started again for this summer.'

'This may sound irrelevant to you, but would Lucifer's brother know for some weeks ahead that Lucifer would be with him last week-end?'

'Oh yes. The relatives affected were informed months ago about the start of the holiday season. We call it the holiday season.'

'Do you keep letters from relatives? Letters to the hospital I mean, not letters to the patients.'

'Why do you ask that?'

'Gabriel, that's Lucifer's brother, he moves around a lot. He has a caravan, you know. I'm wondering if he has kept the hospital posted about where he was staying from time to time.'

'And if he has?' Miss Armstrong was getting tired of answering questions which seemed pointless to her.

Martineau kept the edge out of his voice. It would have been grossly unfair for him to blast off at this obliging person. 'If he has, I want to know the various places he's stayed at while he's been in correspondence with the hospital,' he said. 'He's a criminal. He's in custody right now, for committing at least two serious crimes in this police district during the past seven days. If you want to know how serious these crimes are, one of them is murder. I shall want to know his various stopping places in the hope of clearing other crimes which he has committed.'

There was silence.

'Are you still there?' Martineau asked gently.

'Yes, sir,' the girl said in a small voice.

'I have worse news than that. We think that *Lucifer* committed at least one serious crime while he was at liberty last week-end, and we are now seeking him for a crime he committed today, on the outskirts of this city.'

'Oh,' Miss Armstrong breathed.

'Who is the man in charge at Lambham Hall? The top man of all?'

'Dr. Lorraine.' The girl might have been pronouncing the name of her deity.

'Perhaps you'd better put me through to him.'

'*I* couldn't do that!'

'Somebody can, I suppose.'

'Will you hold the line, please?'

'No,' said Martineau. 'This is long distance.' His instinct was to push the inquiry relentlessly, while the opposition was in confusion, but he knew that he would have to wait for Dr. Lorraine anyway. Once this girl had put down the telephone, she would not pick it up again until the doctor's secretary or assistant, and afterwards the doctor, had heard the full story, and spoken with the worried Miss Giles, and decided what had better be said to the police. There was no sense in holding the line until all that had transpired.

'Have you got a pencil?' he asked, and when the girl replied he said: 'The number here is Central 1212, and my name is Martineau. I expect to hear from Dr. Lorraine in half an hour or less. You must make sure he understands that if I don't hear from him, I shall ask my Chief Constable to get in touch with the Home Office. Is that clear?'

'Yes, sir,' the girl whispered, and she rang off without staying to say good-bye.

'What a profession,' said Martineau as he put down the receiver; and he was referring, without reverence, to his own.

.          .          .          .          .

Inside the half-hour Dr. Lorraine's call came through to Martineau, and it came in a manner which always irritated him. Some female underling got through to him and told him that the doctor wished to converse, and then he counted the seconds by his watch for nearly a minute before he heard the man's voice.

'Chief Inspector Martineau?'

'Yes. Dr. Lorraine?'

'In person. What seems to be the trouble?'

'So we're going to be offhand about it,' the policeman thought. He said: 'Have you spoken with Miss Armstrong?'

'Yes. It seems to me that she answered all your questions.'

'So we're taking the offensive, too,' Martineau thought. He made a mental picture of the man with whom he was talking. It was of course a man accustomed to giving orders, and taking them seldom. His orders were never questioned. He was a smooth talker and probably a good talker. He sounded as if he might be witty, and he was bound to be learned and sure to be intelligent. But he talked down to Martineau, a chief inspector of police who had him at a disadvantage. So he had yet to prove to Martineau that he was not a fool.

'She answered most of my questions, Doctor, but I have more to ask. She isn't the one to answer them. You are. You or Miss Giles.'

'She's rather under the weather at the moment.'

'Taking cover there, no doubt. Have you talked with her about this business of Lucifer Lavengro?'

'Er, yes. I have.' With that brief utterance Lorraine's tone changed almost imperceptibly. He was no longer talking down. He was getting ready to talk on behalf of a subordinate. Perhaps he had the virtue of loyalty to his staff.

'I want to know what that woman thinks she's playing at,' Martineau said bluntly. 'Why did she lie to me when I asked her if Lucifer was at liberty last week-end?'

'She did wrong,' Lorraine admitted, and now he had swung still further towards conciliation. 'She's an excellent soul, the best almoner I ever had, and she really has the interests of the patients at heart.' The doctor made his sigh audible. 'A little too much at heart in this case.'

'After she put me off with that falsehood, did she just let it go? Didn't she do *anything*?'

Lorraine became downright apologetic. 'As a matter of fact she did. She questioned Lucifer, and asked him if he'd been misbehaving during the week-end. He said he'd been as good as gold, and she believed him. No, don't say it. I know. But she's a woman dedicated to the patients. She just thought that the police had made a mistake.'

'You mean she thinks the mentally degenerate patients are wonderful, and the police are a lot of blundering idiots?'

'Steady, Inspector. You can't sum the matter up like that. Miss Giles has a wonderful record. She's done a lot of good work over and above the requirements of her position. I suppose she knows nothing about the police, and has a mistaken opinion of them. But she does know the patients. She regards them as children. Most of them are mentally retarded, and they respond like children to treatment.'

'Rather dangerous children, aren't they?'

'Some of them, yes. Most of them are as quiet as mice.'

'As a patient, is Lucifer as quiet as a mouse?'

'Yes, you could say so. He has always been docile.'

'He's been kidding you. *He's* about as docile as a rogue elephant. I *know* that, and I've never set eyes on him. As for his insanity, I don't know. This afternoon he attacked a young woman in a way which may or may not have been insane, but when he became in danger of capture he desisted and got out of there quick. He had so much control. And he knew what he was doing, and he knew it was wrong.'

'M'Naghten's ruling isn't regarded as decisive these days, you know.'

'Perhaps not. But when we get hold of him he'll have to prove his insanity all over again before we let go of him. And as for Miss Giles, she may have done a lot of good work, and she may have been kidded by a few crafty nuts like Lucifer. She may be in love with the man without being aware of it. He's handsome, you know. But apart from that, her opinion of the police convinces me she isn't normal. Because I made a simple inquiry about Lucifer she immediately jumped to the conclusion that the police were harrying every poor defective who was anywhere near this city last week-end. To protect Lucifer she lied to me, with the result that a dangerous criminal is now at liberty when he should have been under lock and key. She's dedicated all right.'

Lorraine thought he had heard the worst, and he was beginning to think that there was not a great deal to worry about. 'You make it sound very serious, Inspector,' he said. 'I hope you're not making it more serious than it really is. Today Lucifer lost his head, and there was an abortive assault on a young woman, is that it?'

'That's it,' said Martineau with irony. 'There is a little more which hardly seems worth mentioning. Last Saturday night he broke into the house of a maiden lady—she actually was a maiden, by the way—and raped her. Later the same night, in my belief, he murdered a woman by cutting her throat. If you read a newspaper you may know something about that.'

'Oh dear.' Dr. Lorraine was very thoughtful indeed. 'You have evidence?'

'I have some evidence, and I hope to have more when I get hold of Lucifer. I'm going to send a man to see you, to collect all Lucifer's clothes. I mean his own, not the ones which he wears in hospital.'

'I'll see that your man gets everything, though I believe Lucifer has just one suit of his own. Most of those allowed leave have just one outfit.'

'I'll want all his boots and shoes. Every pair.'

'Of course, if you want them.'

'When I lay this murder on Lucifer, there's going to be an awful uproar. There'll be questions in Parliament. How are you fixed at that end?'

Lorraine knew quite well what Martineau meant, but he played for time. 'In what way?'

'As regards authority to let people out on leave. Is there a Home Office order?'

'It's been the custom for years to let certain patients out of mental hospitals from time to time.'

'Ordinary mental hospitals, yes. And voluntary patients, I guess. But your patients are criminals.'

'I assure you that this place has been run according to regulations.'

'Well, you should know. And it's your funeral. I shall put in a report about Miss Giles, of course.'

'Are you compelled to do that?'

'I'm going to do it. If she has a wonderful record, she can trot it out in her own defence at the Home Office inquiry. She's made a sickening lot of work and worry for me and my men, not to mention one policewoman who might very easily have been murdered.'

'Look. Miss Giles will write to you and apologize.'

'I don't want her to do that. That wouldn't change her way of thinking.'

'And would a Home Office inquiry?'

'Perhaps not. But it would make her a bit more careful in dealing with police inquiries. We have enough on our plates without having to suffer from the prejudices of female cranks in authority.'

'Those are not the words of a gentleman, Inspector.'

'You can't be a policeman and a gentleman both,' said Martineau. 'I gave up trying a long time since.'

## NINETEEN

WHEN Martineau glanced through Lewis Badger's ready reckoner he failed to find any indication that it was used for an ulterior purpose, so he started at the front cover and scrutinized each page. The book was of fine india paper and he had to be careful that he did not miss a page. He nearly missed pages 40 and 41, and discovered that they had been stuck together with a spot of gum no bigger than a pinhead. Many numbers on page 40 had been underlined in ink, apparently in a haphazard fashion. He dialled a number on the internal-line telephone and spoke to Detective Chief Superintendent Clay.

'Have we such a thing as a cipher expert on the force, sir?' he asked.

'Not to my knowledge,' Clay replied.

'Thank you,' said Martineau. He rang off, and sent for the man who had brought the ready reckoner to him.

'Go back to Badger's place and bring me every book and every newspaper,' he said. 'I want every bit of printed matter he's got: books, newspapers, travel guides, pamphlets, the lot. If he's got any shelves lined with newspaper, I want them too. I also want every bit of correspondence you can find, including telegrams and cablegrams.'

The man went away, and Martineau continued his examination of the ready reckoner. He found that pages 50 and 51, 60 and 61, 70 and 71 and 80 and 81 were gummed together. Pages 50, 60, 70 and 80 were marked in ink, not exactly as page 40 was marked, but in a similar manner. Also, ten pages from the end of the book, he found two more pages gummed together and marked.

He sent for Badger, preferring to hold the preliminary

interview in his own office rather than the windowless interrogation-room, simply because the sun was shining and he liked it. He left the ready reckoner on the desk.

Badger took his seat on the opposite side of the desk. Martineau remained silent for some time, as if in thought. Badger saw the little book, and thereafter was careful not to look at it.

'Yes, it's yours,' said Martineau. 'It seems to contain some sort of a code. We won't be long cracking it. We have experts, you know.'

'Am I under arrest?' Badger demanded.

'I've just decided that you are, because I shall have to hold you. Therefore I caution you that you need not say anything in answer to my questions, but that anything you do say will be taken down in writing and may be given in evidence.'

'What's the charge?'

'One of the charges will be accessary after the fact of a felony. That'll do for bringing you up in front of the Stipendiary in the morning and holding you on remand.'

'You've got no evidence.'

Martineau tapped the ready reckoner. 'I have evidence, and I will have more,' he said.

'What evidence do you have?'

'Verbal evidence is part of it. The only part I'm ready to talk about. On second thoughts, I don't think I want to talk about that, either.'

'You mean I've been shopped?'

'I haven't said so.'

'You've been talking to Tiffany, I know that. Anything he says isn't evidence against me.'

'Tiffany isn't the only one we've got in custody.'

'You could have a dozen. It's got nothing to do with me.'

'Gabriel murdered Herbie,' said Martineau as if he were passing on a piece of gossip.

Badger stared. 'I don't believe it,' he said, but it was obvious that he did.

Martineau shrugged. 'Why would I say it if it weren't so?

He murdered Herbie, and we've got him right. We've had the whole lot of you under observation for some time. He buried Herbie on the moors, and we went and dug him up.'

Badger thought about that. 'How did he kill him?' he asked.

'Poisoned with an oversize injection of cocaine. Did him in his sleep.'

Badger shuddered. 'I'm glad I'm clear of that,' he said. Martineau made a mental note that he did not ask about Gabriel's motive for murder. Probably he had a very good idea about that.

'While he's trying to get out from under the murder job he might cough up something about the drug affair,' Martineau said hopefully. 'We've got him right on that, too.'

'If he gets tried for murder it'll be one thing at a time. There'll be no talk about drugs.'

'Oh yes, there will. It's bound to be brought into it. It covers both the motive and the opportunity.'

'Ah well,' said Badger. 'It's got nothing to do with me.'

'I was thinking you might explain this code to me, and save me a lot of trouble.'

'I know nothing about any code.'

'I thought you'd say that, but there was no harm in trying. What were your relations with Tiffany?'

'I know him by sight.'

'You know him better than that. You know Gabriel too, and you knew Herbie. We've got you taped. You've been watched, I tell you.'

'So what?'

'So you're getting a chance to be helpful. It might be your last chance. What were your relations with Tiffany? Was he your boss, or were you his?'

'You're wasting your time.'

'I believe I am,' Martineau agreed. He turned to the detective who stood by the door. 'Take this man into the charge-room. I'll be along there in a little while.'

.      .      .      .      .

When the books and papers arrived from Badger's lodging, Martineau looked at them with distaste, and then he spoke on the intercom to Sergeant Bird, the force's chief fingerprint officer.

'Do you know anything about codes and ciphers?' he asked.

'I once read a book about them,' Bird admitted cautiously.

'Good,' said Martineau heartily. 'I knew we'd have an expert somewhere. Come along to my office, will you? I have a little job for you.'

Bird came along. He entered the office with a defensive air. Badger had more than a hundred books, some of them well used, and in addition there was an untidy pile of miscellaneous literature. When Bird saw them he said: 'I'm no expert, sir.'

'You seem to be the only one we've got,' said Martineau, who had a great respect for Bird's mental ability. 'There's no need for you to cart all this stuff away. I'll help you to find the key document, and then you can take it away and crack the cipher. When you've done that, we'll see what we can find among these letters.'

Bird was shown the marked pages in the ready reckoner. He studied them, and Martineau saw him grow interested. Then he turned to the books. 'Is there a Holy Bible among this lot?' he asked.

The Bible was found and put on one side. Bird also picked out *Whitaker's Almanack*, the works of William Shakespeare, a dictionary, and the only volume of Dickens, *Dombey and Son*.

'I'll take these for a start,' he said. He looked at the miscellany. 'What's this lot?'

'Newspapers, pamphlets and such. A newspaper could be used, couldn't it?'

'What are all these odd pages?'

Martineau looked at the man who had brought the books. The man said: 'Those were lining the drawers in Badger's dressing-table and wardrobe.'

'H'm.' Bird picked up the sheets of newspaper and began to look through them. He stopped momentarily, staring at the date of one of them. Martineau also noticed the date. The paper was a section of *The Times* of January 1st six years ago. He concealed a smile as Bird quickly folded the papers and said: 'I may as well take these, too.'

When Bird had gone, Martineau looked at his watch. The time was six o'clock within a few minutes; time to end a normal day's work. He sighed and stretched. He was tired, hungry and thirsty, but by no means depressed. The Gabriel–Lucifer mystery had solved itself and the hunt was up for Lucifer. There was a chance of clearing the one outstanding crime, the murder of Ella Bowie. There *might* be a chance of breaking up a dope ring entirely. Matters could have been worse, and had been many a time.

The chief inspector went into the charge-room and attended to the legal locking-up of Lewis Badger, then he went out of the building and across the road, in search of half an hour's relaxation, a sandwich and a pint of beer.

.            .            .            .            .

When he returned to his office, Martineau began to sort the correspondence of Lewis Badger. This, apparently, had never been profuse. The policeman soon sifted what he called 'the wheat from the chaff'. He was left in possession of some three dozen letters covering a period of about five years. The letters were significant, but unless some startling discoveries were made elsewhere, they would not be of much value as evidence. All of them were typewritten. They were dated, but they bore no addresses. Probably each one had been sent *poste restante* and the envelope destroyed. All of them were headed 'Dear Sir' and signed by various single names which were obviously code names. Some of them were written in very odd English, and some were written in Spanish. They were business letters, but references to 'goods', prices and payments were guarded.

The letters made Martineau ponder about Badger. The

man was obviously the organizer and paymaster of the Granchester cell of the gang, and possibly he was even more important than that. Very likely he had been the brains behind the British Medicaments robbery. The chief inspector made notes of the inquiries he would have to make. He would require court orders to ascertain how wealthy was the modest Mr. Badger. There would be money, valuables, deeds and securities in various banks and safe deposits. The quiet Mr. Badger might even be a substantial owner of property and real estate. Without doubt it was time he retired. If the police did not succeed in putting him entirely out of business, and out of circulation for a long number of years, justice would not have been done.

'At least five years he's been at it, right under my nose,' Martineau muttered.

Then Sergeant Bird returned, looking pleased with himself. 'A simple cipher, but a stinker,' he announced. 'I thought he had me beat once over.'

'You found the clue in the January first issue of *The Times*?'

'Yes. That looked suspicious, being the only bit of *The Times* in the whole collection. The lad who found it lining a drawer ought to be congratulated.'

Martineau nodded. And since it is not good police procedure for an officer to allow his own sagacity to go unnoticed he said: 'That was my idea.'

Bird grinned. 'Congratulations,' he said.

'Thanks. What did you get out of the code?'

'Names and addresses. But first I got nothing but gibberish. But I had faith in *The Times*. The marked colume in the ready reckoner was the same column in the leader page. The first digit of a number from ten to a hundred, or the first and second digit of a number in the hundreds, meant the number of lines down the column, exclusive of headlines. The second digit, or the third digit, or the third and fourth as the case may be, meant the number of letters along the line. The sequence was obtained by following the marks, irrespective of relative position otherwise, from the bottom to the top of the page. I tried it both ways, up and down, and got nothing but rubbish. Then I turned to that page near the end, and I happened to notice that there were only fifty-two marks on the page. That was it.'

'A code within a code?'

'A code for a cipher,' said Bird. 'It all worked out, twenty-six numbers representing letters, with twenty-six opposite numbers. Against number one you have fourteen, so that A in the code was really the fourteenth letter, N. That was the key, and if I hadn't found it, it would have taken me a hell of a long time to decipher the thing.'

'Could you have done it without the key?'

'I think so, eventually. But foreign names and addresses wouldn't have made it any easier. Why on earth did he leave the key in the same book as the cipher examples?'

'I suppose he didn't think anybody would notice a few marks in a book. He was right, too. It just so happens that I was told to look for them.'

'I see. Well, here are your names and addresses as near as I could get them.'

Martineau studied the list. There were fifteen names, of men living in Istanbul, Beirut, Haifa, Alexandria, Tangier, Paris, Antwerp, London, New York, Philadelphia, New Orleans, Caracas, Rio de Janeiro, São Paulo and Buenos Aires. Names and addresses too many and too strange for Badger to have committed to memory. It was obvious now that he, living so quietly in a northern English city, was the central operator, postman, or liaison officer of a large network dealing illicitly in narcotics. Yes indeed, Mr. Badger would have to be put away.

'What will you do with that lot?' Bird wanted to know.

Martineau rose to his feet, with the list in his hands. 'Somebody's going to hear about your good work,' he said. 'I'll have to see Clay, and he'll probably send me to talk to the Chief Constable, whatever he happens to be doing. I might have to send off a flock of cablegrams, or

I might have to bung the whole lot of this off to Interpol.'

'Or both,' Bird suggested.

'Or both,' the other agreed. 'Whatever we do, there won't have to be so much time wasted. When we've sent off our information we'll just have to wait and hope that some honest copper in some far city finds some evidence against our Mr. Badger.'

'And is kind enough to notify us.'

'We can pray for that, too.'

'These names might be the means of wrapping up the whole organization, lock, stock and barrel.'

'Now you're in the realms of fantasy,' said Martineau.

# TWENTY

FRIDAY NIGHT and most of Saturday passed without news of Lucifer Lavengro. Martineau's prisoners were 'had up' and remanded in custody while further police inquiries could be made. There were further interviews with the prisoners, but no further information from them. Tiffany was jumpy and apprehensive, Badger was calm but worried, Gabriel was impassive. When Martineau told him about the hunt for Lucifer, he smiled and shrugged.

'How will you know he's Luce when you get him?' he asked. 'He might be Gabriel.'

'What good do you think that gag might do you?' the policeman wanted to know.

'Gag? You don't know who I am.'

'I'll settle it all right when I have the pair of you, and then I'll put labels on you. The Bristol Police should have fingerprints of Luce.'

'I don't think so. He was insane, you know.'

'You're the man who wrote that letter to Lambham Hall. Luce couldn't have done it. His writing won't be the same as yours.'

'Still, I might be Luce. We've changed places at Lambham Hall before today.'

'They'll have specimens of Luce's writing at Lambham Hall. And I don't believe you've ever taken Luce's place there. You couldn't take a chance on Luce behaving himself when he was passing as Gabriel. If you took Luce's place at Lambham you risked spending the rest of your life there.'

'Luce does exactly what Gabriel tells him.'

'All right, but I'll sort you out. The one who wears

Luce's boots will swing for the murder of Ella Bowie, and
the one who wears Gabriel's will go down for the murder
of Herbie Small. Now get back to your cell and see if you
can dream up something else.'

After that talk, Martineau sat brooding about Lucifer.
He wanted the man to be caught in his own police district,
but if that wish was not granted, he supposed the arrest
would be made the following day at Lambham Hall,
before the wanted man could get back on to hospital
premises. Unless he remembered Miss Giles's questions
and formed a surmise from them, Lucifer would assume
that the police did not know him as an inmate of Lambham
Hall. Miss Giles had not told him that the police had been
inquiring about him, she had merely asked him if he had
been a good boy while on his week-end pass. So he would
be hiding and hoping that he could evade arrest until he
could return to Lambham at the usual time. At Lambham
he would expect to be safe from the police.

Sergeant Devery and Policewoman Valentine also
considered the problem of Lucifer as they prowled in the
Jaguar on Saturday afternoon.

'For the murder of Ella Bowie he's the only runner in
Martineau's stable,' Devery said. 'If he turns out to be a
non-murdering lunatic he'll be a great disappointment.'

'Is there much chance of that?'

'Not since you found the razor, my little chickadee. It
had been cleansed, but the back-room boys discovered
traces of blood inside the handle. The blood is human, of
the same group as poor Ella's.'

'That should help.'

'Yes. But the shoes and trouser-bottoms, and possibly
other parts of clothing, will tell the tale when we get them.
Luce won't have destroyed his suit. Before he met you
yesterday he was too secure. Since then he won't have had
the chance. Probably he still doesn't know he's wanted
for murder, anyway.'

It was a quiet afternoon, with no bright ideas from
anybody until six o'clock, when the two prowlers were

having a light meal. It was a sign of their closer relation-
ship that they sat together at a table in the canteen. Then
it was that Rosamund suddenly remarked: 'Apropos of
Lucifer, I wonder how Miss Naylor is getting on.'

Devery stared at her. He was awed by the idea she had
suggested. 'Jesus,' he breathed. 'He wouldn't dare go back
there!'

'Why not? He might think he's welcome. His mind isn't
supposed to work like other people's.'

'We could make a friendly phone call, to ask her if she's
now quite well and all that.'

Rosamund put down a half-eaten sandwich. 'I'll go
and ring now,' she said. 'I'll use one of those through lines
in the C.I.D.'

She was gone five minutes, and when she returned she
was pale and tense.

'Miss Naylor's phone is dead, quite dead,' she said.

Devery frowned. 'You're sure?'

'I tried. Then I dialled Nine-One and asked the girl to
try. The line was dead.'

The sergeant sat in thought. 'Maybe those phone
wires are cut,' he said. 'That was quite a notion you had,
Policewoman Valentine. We'd better have a word with
Martineau.'

'Why?'

Again he stared at her in surprise. Then he said: 'Lucifer
is a heavyweight, a wrestler, and a madman. Are you
suggesting that you and I alone should try to take him?'

The girl was still very pale. 'Why not? *You're* a heavyweight, aren't you?'

'Just about,' he admitted. 'But I couldn't be at the back
and front of the house as well.'

'I could take the back. I could hold him long enough for
you to get on the scene.'

'But you're scared to death already, at the very thought
of Lucifer.'

'Never mind about that. I want us to tackle it.'

'He'd brush you aside like a cobweb.'

195

'No, he wouldn't.'

'You want to have another go at him, to prove something to yourself, don't you?'

'Yes, I want to prove something. I hate him. He's just a leering beast. I want to show I'm not afraid, and I want to prove that you can take him. You and I, anyway.'

Devery pretended to be astonished. 'Why me?'

She looked at him and he had his answer. Then she said: 'You've got to be a better man than he is.'

'Phew,' he said. 'That's a tall order.'

'Are you scared?'

'Certainly I'm scared. If he slips us, I might lose my stripes. All right, young woman, we'll have a go. Finish your tea.'

'I don't want it. Let's go now.'

Devery glanced out of the window. Then he studied Rosamund's taut face. 'Here, have a cigarette and relax,' he said. 'By the time we get to Miss Naylor's place it'll be half-dark. That's no good. We'll let it get properly dark. He'll be coming out of a lighted house. Such an advantage is legitimate, I think.'

.     .     .     .     .

As the Jaguar stopped in Edgley Crescent, Devery pocketed the ignition key and remarked crisply: 'What a sell if he isn't here.'

That was all. Policeman and policewoman walked up to Miss Naylor's front door, and the man rang the bell. When it was not immediately answered, he rang again. The girl stood back a little, and to one side. She could see the gate of the little back garden, and she could also look up at the lighted, but curtained, bedroom window. She saw a shadow near the side of the window, but she could not see enough of it to determine the shape or size of the person who made it. The curtain moved a little where the shadow was.

Devery tried the door. It was locked. Then Miss Naylor

196

could be heard on the other side of the door. 'Who is there?' she called rather breathlessly.

'Sergeant Devery and Policewoman Valentine,' the sergeant replied. 'We just want to know if you're all right.'

'Oh yes.' Miss Naylor certainly was breathless. 'I'm quite all right. You'll—excuse me if I don't open the door. I'm not dressed.'

'That's all right,' said Devery. 'We'll wait.'

'What's that?'

'We've got to see you,' Rosamund called clearly. 'We'll wait until you're dressed.'

'Oh, all right,' the woman replied.

Then, when the impression had been given that the two people who had called were both waiting at the front door, Rosamund faded silently along the side of the house to the back. When she arrived there she saw that the light was on in the kitchen. The kitchen window had thin curtains of flowered material, and through them the small back lawn was bathed in light. She moved across the lawn and took her stand about five yards from the door and to the side of it. In that position she was not directly in the light from the window, and she was in the shadow of a well-grown laburnum tree which stood near the fence on that side. She was also handily on the flank of anybody who might emerge from the kitchen and go towards the front gate.

Her face was set and pale. When she began to tremble she breathed deeply, as she had been taught, to keep her nerves relaxed.

The kitchen light went out, and the door was slightly opened. A big man came out. He set off a-tiptoe towards the back gate, without bothering to close the door behind him. Rosamund darted out of the shadow and went for him, and all he could have seen of her then was a flash of movement. As she had expected, a big hand came out in an instinctive hand-off movement. She seized the thick wrist in her two small hands and pulled, while still going towards her antagonist. She had the advantage of catching

197

him while he was balanced on his toes. She cried: 'Hup!' as if she were addressing a performing animal, and in a flicker of movement she executed a sort of turning curtsey as she danced under the arm she held. The man's height made this easy for her, and he could not turn with her because she was too quick for him. Then she was behind his back, and the arm she held was twisted behind him. The whole movement, so far, had taken about two-fifths of a second.

Rosamund was not so optimistic as to imagine that she could hold Luce Lavengro with his arm behind his back. She was still in motion, intent on achieving a throw. With a flat-heeled shoe she kicked as hard as she could at the back of his knee, pulling backward at the same time. He was hard to throw. Instead of falling, he staggered, but the kick prevented him from acquiring enough balance to turn. She had expected that he would be hard to throw, and she did not hesitate for a moment. Her feet were in constant twinkling movement. Still pulling, she kicked again. Luce fell, and she did not release his wrist until she was sure that he would fall on his back.

He rolled over with astonishing agility, and he would have been on his feet in a moment. But she had anticipated that also. She took a short run and jumped as high as she could, and as he was raising himself on hands and knees she landed with both heels in the small of his back. He grunted and went flat, but he was rising again when someone said: 'Right.' Rosamund got out of the way as Devery arrived. He landed with both knees and all his hundred and ninety pounds on the spot where the girl's heels had been a moment before. That crash landing completely deflated Luce.

'Here,' said Rosamund, and handcuffs were thrust at Devery. It is not done in British police circles to shackle a man's hands behind his back. It is strictly not the thing to do. But Devery made an exception of Luce.

.    .    .    .    .

Devery left Rosamund with Miss Naylor while he took Luce to Headquarters and left him in the willing hands of Martineau. From Headquarters he telephoned Dr. Lindsay, and when he got back to Edgley Crescent to pick up his partner he met Lindsay there. The unfortunate woman was already in bed with a sedative. The doctor said that she would be all right, and that he had sent for a friend of hers to come and stay with her.

Devery and Rosamund departed. The sergeant wanted to get back to the C.I.D. where, he presumed, things were happening. He was jubilant. 'We've got Lucifer right,' he said. 'Martineau had the pants off him before he'd been in the place five minutes. Blood on his pants. Shoes, blood. Coat, blood. Not obvious, but there all the same. But the best bit of evidence of the lot was a brooch of Ella's which he still had in his pocket. It must have taken his fancy. I'll bet Gabriel didn't know he had it. If Martineau can't crack him with that lot, I'll eat this steering wheel.'

There was some further talk about Gabriel, Lucifer, Badger and Co., and then Devery asked: 'How *was* Miss Naylor?'

'Not so shaken as you'd think. She seemed to have got used to the idea of Luce being there, but she cheered up a lot when she knew we had him under arrest.'

'When did he get in? And how?'

'Last night, soon after dark. She had the doors locked but he waited round the back until she took something out to the bin, and then he walked in. She was too paralysed with fright to do anything, she said. He got a knife and cut the telephone adrift, and then he told her he was staying until Sunday afternoon. He said no harm would come to her if she behaved herself. He got her word of honour on that, and pretended to give her a sort of parole. But she said he watched her like a hawk just the same.'

'Did he . . . er . . . ?'

Rosamund smiled in the darkness of the car. 'I couldn't quite frame the question myself,' she said. 'I asked her if

199

she wanted to make a fresh charge on any account at all, and she said "No". She was emphatic about it.'

'So that's something we'll never know, unless Luce starts boasting about it. We won't know whether he's telling the truth, anyway.'

'Anyway, he didn't knock her about or threaten her with a knife. She confessed to me that she thought he rather liked her.'

'Would you credit it? And was she getting fond of Luce?'

'I didn't have the impertinence to ask.'

'It takes all sorts to make a world. She might have happy memories of him.'

'Exciting ones, perhaps,' Rosamund admitted. Then she said sharply: 'How could she? He's horrible!'

## TWENTY-ONE

THE following day Rosamund paraded for duty at two
o'clock carrying her report, which she had written at
home. It was a modest document. She merely stated that
she had visited Edgley Crescent in company with Sergeant
Devery, and had assisted in the arrest of Lucifer Lavengro,
and after that paragraph she had given only the necessary
details of her interview with Miss Naylor.

She found that Devery had been at Headquarters all
morning, completing his paper work, helping with interrogation, and generally trying to get all the information
he could. He had succeeded in getting most of what was
available.

The two began the last tour of duty of their fortnight
on the prowl, and Devery drove. 'You've done so well,'
he said, 'that I wouldn't like you to spoil your C.I.D.
record by having a bump.'

Rosamund looked through the windscreen at an empty
Sunday street and said: 'You watch what *you're* doing, and
while you're about it you can tell me what has happened
since last night.'

'Martineau is pleased with everybody, including Lucifer,'
the sergeant replied. 'So far there's been just one reply to
his messages up and down the world. London; the Metro-
politan Police District. The Metro have twenty-four hours'
advantage either way on any of the others, of course. They
phoned this morning. The address he gave them was a
so-called Seamen's Hostel in Limehouse. Chinese seamen,
and pseudo seamen. It seems they've been watching it for
some time, with not much satisfaction. So when they
received Martineau's tip they got rolling and raided the

201

place. They found a lot of opium and some likely-looking correspondence, both in Chinese and very queer English. Martineau is hoping there'll be something which will involve Badger. It's made him a lot more hopeful about the other addresses, too.'

'What about Lucifer?'

'Martineau spent half the night with him. First of all he let him know how Ella's brooch could hang him. He had a few bloodstained pound notes which were probably hers, but the brooch makes it a certain case of murder in the furtherance of theft. That didn't move him much until Martineau convinced him that Gabriel hadn't a chance of getting clear of the full responsibility for Herbie's murder. When Lucifer was sure that he couldn't make things either better or worse for Gabriel, he started thinking about himself. It didn't seem to occur to him to wait and let a lawyer do his thinking for him, and maybe he was right, because according to Martineau he saw his problem clear enough. He had two things to do. Do his best to get out of it by still being considered insane, or, failing that, get from under the capital charge by discrediting the "furtherance of theft" motive.'

'Won't he automatically be judged insane, if he was certified and on leave from a mental hospital?'

'No. He'll be tried for murder, and during the trial the question of his insanity will be considered all over again. He may know that, because he's seeking safety by playing it both ways. Of course he had to come clean, or fairly clean.'

'So he's told all?'

'More or less. Ella was murdered because she happened to see Gabriel and Lucifer together. They met only for two minutes in the street, and that was due to a misunderstanding of Gabriel's orders. Ella passed on her way home. She saw them and they saw her. Herbie was present, and Herbie said: "That dame talks to cops." The danger was obvious.'

'Of course. Ella might have mentioned the remarkable

likeness to you even if she didn't have the possibility of crime in her mind.'

'That is so, and now we come to a part of the story where Luce seems to stray from the strict truth. He says Herbie reminded him that it was his fault he had been seen with Gabriel, and that Herbie told him to go after her and kill her. He says that Gabriel wouldn't agree to murder, and that he was overruled. So he went after Ella, got ahead of her and waylaid her, with poor dead Herbie accessary before the fact and Gabriel nicely in the clear. He says that robbery wasn't in his mind, that somebody else must have taken Ella's money, that he picked up the brooch because it fell to the ground, and that he was going to return it anonymously to Ella's people when he found out who they were.'

'Is the brooch valuable?'

'No. Worth a few shillings. He has a reasonable chance. of persuading a jury that robbery was not in his mind when he committed murder.'

'And what about his insanity plea?'

'I don't think he has a cat-in-hell chance, though you never can tell. He's too lucid about motive, and of course he has to be if he wants to get away from the capital charge.'

'The horns of a dilemma.'

'Yes. He's cleared up the rape job all right. He says Herbie was with him, and that it was Herbie's idea. He says Gabriel knew nothing about it.'

'What about the B.M. job?'

'He brings Gabriel into that, probably thinking he's whitewashed him enough. He and Gabriel did it, and Herbie waited somewhere in the car. It was Gabriel, not Luce, who bowled you over and made me measure my length in the street.'

'Does he say anything about Tiffany and Badger?'

'He doesn't know Tiffany, but he's met Badger. He doesn't care two hoots about Badger, but unfortunately he can't give us any testimony concerning him. He *knows* that Badger was present when the rape and the B.M.

jobs were planned, but he wasn't present himself. Dammit, I wish Herbie was alive. We'd get Badger right if he was.'

'And Gabriel too; that's why Herbie was killed.'

'We've got Gabriel right as it is.'

'So that's the lot, up to press?'

'Yes, and a nice little lot it is. Oh, there's Knight Lancelot Green's brief-case. He's identified it. Gabriel won't have any of it and of course Luce was inside at the time. Anyway, the Bristol police are going to write the job off with Gabriel's name in the margin.'

Devery stared ahead dreamily. 'We seem to work very well as a team, you and I,' he said. 'There'll be some nice little commendation over this affair. You'll do better than me in that respect.'

'I want you to get the commendations,' said Rosamund, also dreamy. 'You'll need them.'

'The man of the family, you mean?'

'You said it, I didn't.'

'It isn't your place to say such things, and methinks I might have been unduly rash.'

'Don't worry. You haven't put yourself in danger.'

'I didn't mean that. I risked a rebuff. Come to think of it, I got one. But I don't think our association will end today. I think it's just beginning.'

Rosamund did not deny that, and there was a contented silence in the car.

Then Devery said: 'Your little idea about tackling Lucifer didn't prove anything.'

'We took him, didn't we?'

'*You* did. He was taking a count when I came on the scene. All I had to do was jump on him. How on earth did you manage to get him down?'

'It's a trick that isn't in the book,' said Rosamund. 'I used to practise it on nasty little boys when I was a sweet little girl.'

'I'm glad I didn't go to your school,' said Devery.

>>> If you've enjoyed this book and would like to discover more great vintage crime and thriller titles, as well as the most exciting crime and thriller authors writing today, visit: >>>

## The Murder Room
**Where Criminal Minds Meet**

**themurderroom.com**